us

By the same author

The Complete Guide to London's Antique Street Markets
Nineteenth Century Romantic Bronzes
Under the Hammer: The Auctions and Auctioneers of London
Dealing with Dealers: The Ins and Outs of the London Antiques Trade
Ruth
Victorian and Edwardian Furniture and Interiors

US

JEREMY COOPER

Hutchinson
London Sydney Auckland Johannesburg

© *Jeremy Cooper 1990*

All rights reserved

The right of Jeremy Cooper to be identified as Author of this work has been asserted by Jeremy Cooper in accordance with the Copyright, Designs and Patent Act, 1988

This edition first published in 1990 by
Hutchinson

Century Hutchinson Ltd,
20 Vauxhall Bridge Road, London SW1V 2SA

Century Hutchinson Australia
20 Alfred Street, Milsons Point, NSW 2061, Australia

Century Hutchinson New Zealand Limited
PO Box 40–086, Glenfield, Auckland 10, New Zealand

Century Hutchinson South Africa (Pty) Ltd,
PO Box 337, Bergvlei, 2012 South Africa

British Library Cataloguing in Publication Data

Cooper, Jeremy, *1946–*
  Us.
  I. Title
  823'.914 [F]

  ISBN 0–09–173480–0

Photoset in Imprint by Speedset Ltd, Ellesmere Port
Printed and bound in Great Britain by
Butler and Tanner Ltd, Frome, Somerset

us

It's not good enough, not any longer, to claim the words aren't there, to let sentences trickle away into murmurs of ineptitude. My charm is tarnished.

'Who made you?' you used to ask, cupping my cheeks in your hands.

'My parents made me,' I used to reply.

You'd shake your head, and bathe me in smiles. 'No, God did. And gave you to me.'

The Devil, you'd say now.

I must try one last time to sort it out – for myself, here on paper. All the talk, it's driving me insane: the phone-calls, the meetings, the repeated attempts at explanation. Two years of talk and I'm no nearer understanding anything.

If I go back over it all again once more, maybe it will come clear. The awful blackness inside me, the dreadful black thing inside me, eating me up, maybe if I can just catch its tail and pull and pull . . . It'll be dead when I pull it out, dead on the page, I know it will.

And yours? The fat black worm inside you? In killing mine maybe I can kill yours too. Maybe you won't have to take the knife to yours, a stone to crush it head, silence its sucking at our despair.

'You do it. And it's done.' Remember? In *Le Jour Se Lève*. The quickest, most spontaneous of actions; less than action, a re-action only; the instant crack of a reaction set on the move a life-snuffing avalanche of consequences, not just for Jean Gabin, for everyone around.

1

That's how it felt to me. Like in the film. I felt there was nothing I could do to redress the nothing I had done.

I was terribly tired, I remember. A Tuesday. Nothing pressing at work on Tuesdays and I left for home early, tacking from garden hedge to pavement gutter up the hill from the station. I'd intended to call at Roxeth House to check on the Appeal, but felt suddenly exhausted, longed to be home. Gus's city geese honked their habitual warning, I expect. I know I didn't want to see you straight away, and tiptoed past the studio windows.

You weren't in your studio, though. You were in the sitting room, staring at the door – with eyes that didn't seem to see, didn't see the present, anyway. Sitting there overshadowed by the past; shackled to the past, dragging its rusty weight across the carpet behind you.

How did it go exactly?

You started to tell me things, your voice low and indistinct. I couldn't – didn't want to – understand what you were saying.

'What do you mean?'

'The letter,' you replied.

The letter? But I'd torn the letter up. At work. Torn it into tiny squares, envelope and all, and shoved the pieces into a cleaner's plastic sack.

'What letter? I don't know what you mean.'

That did it. You saw red. Purple. Lost control and hurled yourself across the room, reached into a drawer of my desk, grabbed the pages of pink copy paper and waved them in the air. *'This* letter,' I hear you screech across these two – two only? – aching years.

You're good at anger, I envy you the talent. And jealousy. And laughter. And sex. All the passions. I'm better at peace than passion. I hate confrontation, will do anything to escape a quarrel. You said, a week or two later, that you admired my courage in forcing us to confront issues we'd shirked for years. But I wasn't bravely risking our us for the sake of growth, my love, I tell you it never occurred to me that anything like this might happen.

I don't know how it did happen.

Because someone secretly meant it to, you've said. She did. Or I did myself, somehow.

I didn't, you know. I really didn't.

The thing which makes you most angry is that I'm not, and that nothing you can say can make me. It's not that I don't want passion, I do – but not at the price of peace. Peace with passion, passion with peace is what I want, I now understand.

On my walk across the heath (after you'd locked yourself into the studio) I wasn't looking for an explanation, not the true explanation as I am here. It was more a case of reasoning the action away, of negating it. I didn't deny the hurt – couldn't very well: spattered with the blood of your fury – but sought to bind the cut so tight there'd be no scar. Gaping wounds papered over in time by pink films of skin, opened at the merest touch, a nudge from certain memories. I never told you, when I was four, I rolled Sarah-Jane's pushchair over the edge of a step in our garden and she fell out, cracking her head on the flint curb of a flower bed. My father rushed her to York General, where a doctor knotted six stitches in the middle of her taut white forehead. My parents had told me dozens of times to be careful of the pushchair and the step – but I didn't believe them, couldn't believe my little sister would come to harm. Mum said she'd never forgive me if Sarah-Jane was scarred for life. And whilst I knew in my heart the threat would never be carried out, that Mum would forgive me sooner or later whatever I did, I didn't want her to have to. All my life I've wanted to do things so well my mother need have no regrets, ever, where I'm concerned.

I can remember thinking, as I skirted the rows of villas bordering the heath, that I'd made a dreadful mistake: in not following through my adolescent dream of first building a castle and then finding someone to share it with. I remember thinking I'd messed it up, managed it all the wrong way round. You came before the castle, you see. You became my home.

Such a relief: finding you cooking supper in the kitchen when I returned from my walk.

'Not now. Later,' you silenced the opening recital of my lines.

'It's nothing,' you permitted me to reason over coffee. 'I never sent it. She's nothing to me. She's clever and challenging, and I like her young mind. That's all. She's been helpful with the Appeal. That's all.'

I tried to explain to you how Kathy's critical approach to life had inspired my own necessary questioning. I'd been churning out the same stuff at work for years, seduced into repetitive exaggeration by public flattery: I told you. Flattered not only by readers, but colleagues as well. 'Typical Alastair! Got to be different, haven't you?' Kevin Craig-Brown used to remark, with an indulgent upward nod of his editorial head. Different? No. All my articles were exactly the same, different from other people's but in exactly the same way every time. Kathy made me see this – so gentle in rebuke, the truth never seems to hurt. Through knowing her I've recaptured my faith in progress. In everything I do, everything that matters, she's important to me. Vital. I know that. I've never doubted that.

And the letter?

I didn't send it because I realized it might be misinterpreted, I tried to make you understand – sitting together on the Chesterfield one Tuesday evening three Julys ago.

Was it then or another night you came up with the idea that it was ordained to happen?

It's not possible, surely, for a man – a man-and-wife man – to keep the copy of an unsent love-letter in the top drawer of his desk at home, face up, unless fate makes him?

It was good that you found the letter, you said. It would be our saving, you said. Or wrote, I can't remember.

I battled this challenge of yours to our us. There's nothing wrong with us, I pleaded – pathetically no doubt, mouth twitching, words retching. Our us was the basis, the rock of everything. Nothing in the world mattered except us; nothing else mattered at all, compared with us. Without us I didn't exist, I used to be convinced. Without the power behind me of the amazing double person we had created, much larger, much better . . . many times the sum of its separate parts.

How can you doubt us? I asked.

How can you write such a letter? you had the right to question in reply.

Why didn't you? Why didn't you compel me to work it out then instead of waiting till now?

I wish I knew myself, why I kept the carbon copy of a letter never sent. A letter fussed and worried at for days, till the phrases fell into the precise form of telling and not-telling I needed Kathy to understand. Felt sure she would.

Maybe I planned one day to say it to her face and wanted to be reminded of the particular tilt of words, of the secrets whispered between the lines. Those three crinkly pink pages, creased and faded, are in my hands now.

You'd be hurt to know. I know.

I often read the letter – warming to different bits at different times. Today it's this:

> *Remember, at the picnic lunch on my birthday, when I spoke of your sense of balance, your sureness, your joy and beauty (I meant that too, even if I did not say it) and you said that you merely reflected the joys of life, that these qualities were not yours in isolation? Knowing you only with me it is difficult for me to say for sure, but a great deal of what I admire in you seems to be very much yours, not a reflection. Though I think I know what you mean, and am very pleased if, that is, I understand correctly. You are always so honest with yourself – sometimes too critically so. I believe you are also honest with me. Not that there is any need to tell each other everything, not at all – just on important things you need never fear to tell me things you feel the need to tell, even if you are afraid they may bring difficulties or hurt. But again, I am sure you are aware of all that and, like virtually the whole of this letter, it does not need saying.*

'Keep her condescending little comments to yourself,' you said when I told you how much Kathy liked your show at the Galen Gallery.

It's true, Kathy is no match for you, not on your home ground.

We – I – first have to define what the fight is about though, before a victor can be declared.

It's difficult to be certain in what order things – thoughts, particularly – occurred. I'm almost sure I had accepted the commission for the magazine piece on tourist Morocco before you found out about Kathy. When it came to going I know I was so unhappy that I couldn't bear the idea of being alone, of leaving you behind brooding over the letter.

It's stupid to imagine that two people doing together something which one person doesn't wish to do alone will make it any better. We weren't really as feeble as that were we? We used to create something out of nothing, to find genuine worth in everything, didn't we? You especially. You've this wonderful capacity to make the best of things. If we've got to do it it might as well be fun, you'd say. Whilst I'd just mope. Mr Mope, your Aunt Patricia nicknamed me, making me feel worse. Like when I was in a bad mood as a child and my father used to hold up his hands in mock horror. 'Watch out Al! Big black dog on your back! Go on, go away. Naughty dog, off you go,' he'd say, slapping me about the shoulders.

And you? You never seemed to notice my moods. You placed me by your side at the centre of a great circle of optimism, ripples of fun spreading out to touch all in sight.

I dropped in at Roxeth House on the Sunday morning before we left for Agadir. I had to: to tie up with Kathy some loose ends on the Appeal.

I found her coaxing Miss Gaydon into reluctant steps across the rest-room, a whistle dangling on a string from the raggedy-padded grips of Miss Gaydon's zimmer. Kathy looked slightly surprised – but pleased, I felt – at seeing me. 'Come on, show Mr Shore your paces,' she said, and smiled at me, head angled on her beautiful long neck. (Miss Gaydon's neck has retracted into the broken-down trunk of her prematurely ancient body. Her chin rests on her breast-bone.) Miss Gaydon shuffled the couple of yards to her chair. 'Wasn't a no-jump, was it?' she joked, her schoolteacher's humour briefly kindled.

It's clear to me now – was probably just as clear then – that you and Kathy couldn't be more different: her angular precision pitched against your round-limbed exuberance; her hair thick and wavy, yours thin and straight; she tall, you small.

Both of you have brown eyes, bright smiling brown eyes.

'You do it. And it's done.' Gabin's words. There was no going back even if he had wanted to. Where in the story did he cross the point of no return? We reach certain borders and pass into other countries without noticing any change in the landscape. Wars are declared, borders are closed not by us – by you or me, or a Jean Gabin – but by somebody else. Your finding the letter didn't in itself settle anything, necessarily. It was probably settled long ago: perhaps when you declared to me how pretty Kathy was, how she lapped up everything I said. I looked newly at her after you told me that. Maybe you did it . . . Or maybe your mother did. Gus and Fifi are your mother's friends and if she hadn't introduced us to them we'd never have leased their old stables and wouldn't have been living in Blackheath and Fifi wouldn't have persuaded me onto the Board at Roxeth House and I wouldn't have met Kathy, would I? Such a muddle. I can't work it out. Kathy doesn't lap up every word I say anyway, she's very critical. I can't understand how she can be so sure of herself. Twelve years younger than me and she knows exactly what she thinks. When I was twenty-three I didn't know a thing. Except that I had to marry you. That if I married you everything would be all right.

Kathy and I escaped to the office for our chat, seating ourselves either side of my battered municipal desk, summer rain streaming down the bay window.

You remember that funny Mabel I told you about? The woman who dumped herself on the Home's doorstep in a taxi, without papers, doctor's report or anything, and refused to tell Matron where she came from? She used to be Mr Bridge's daily, before he died and left Roxeth House to the Borough . . . *Of course* before he died, what am I writing? Must concentrate. There's got to be a point to everything here or nothing will ever come right . . . What I want to tell you is that Mr Bridge shared the house with a man called Albert Mace, Mabel said. And Mr Mace – Kathy discovered at the Public Records Office – was quite famous in the local way of things, Honorary Life Vice-Chairman of the South

London Magic Circle. We were going to mention him in our new Appeal pamphlet. Another of those timely strokes of fate: that's the point I'm making.

Your finding the letter meant I had to say something to Kathy, in case you mentioned it to her. Not that I felt any obligation to warn Kathy off, to tell her there had been some misunderstanding. Because there hadn't.

I didn't really know what to say.

'Kathy, I'd hate to lose you. Without you the Appeal wouldn't be as successful as it is. Nor would it be half as enjoyable, for me.'

She replied – eyes open enticingly wide, pupils floating free – by saying something about our having done worthwhile work together. I said I hoped she wouldn't be on holiday herself when I returned, and she told me she wasn't going away till September, for a couple of weeks in North Wales. A perfectly ordinary conversation, nothing special.

Then it happened, at the door. She stood at the door with one hand on the knob, but didn't open it. I was standing right beside her, and still she didn't open the door.

So I kissed her on the lips.

Maybe this was the point of no return? Maybe this deliberate touch of my lips to Kathy's was the moment? I did it. Or she did it, by keeping the door closed. Whatever – it was done. The turning point.

Actually, I'd touched her three times before. Misinterpreting each other's intended movements we once collided breast to chest in the main corridor. The second time was at the big desk in the office. Leaning over some papers one afternoon her hair fell into her eyes, and I brushed it back for her with my hand. The third time of touching was when I called at Roxeth House to collect her for our research tour of Brighton nursing homes. I was a few minutes early and her long hair was pinned up on the back of her head from her morning wash. She looked so beautiful, I couldn't resist stroking her neck.

Maybe there never is a precise moment?

I love the way you prepare for holidays. Love the sense of occasion with which you – and your mother – enrich events I knew as a child only for their cold routine.

You Pollards make a joyous ritual of occasions which pass as if unnoticed at home in York. Birthdays, holidays, a midsummer's day picnic, skinny-dipping at full moon, the all-comers, all-weathers Christmas Eve walk through the meadows from Godstow to Christ Church, slower members of the entourage – the youngest hand in hand with the oldest – missing half the Carol Service. You wrap each other's presents in ribbons and coloured tissue, decorate them with cut-out stars and hearts. You Pollards cover parcels in loving messages, and rip them open with cries of delight.

We Shores preserve wrapping paper in a cardboard box at the bottom of the playroom cupboard, the same pock-marked scraps recycled year by year, secured by tiny strips of Sellotape. Sarah-Jane and I learnt never to tear at parcels indiscriminately, but to open them one by one in our appointed corners. All my memories of Christmas presents – the happiest of Uncle Simon's sailing togs and Wilf's yearly Arthur Ransome volumes – are soured by the thank-you letter list. A week was all we were given to complete the list. Proper letters too, no robot replicas, each decreed to contain a pertinent comment on the choice of gift, a paragraph of appropriate school news and a sentence or two about the year's Christmas treat, the form of New Year wishes alone permitted precisely to recur.

It's the women in both our families who set the tone. Our

mothers made us, not God. Not our fathers either. Our fathers provided some of the raw material only.

That's another of the things you object to, isn't it? The idea that I'm my father's son, and might grow old to be like him . . . You're much more a bit of both your parents, in fact, than I am.

We're lucky with our mothers. I may even have loved your mother before I loved you. It's not me who insists you distance yourself from your mother, you know, it's you. Your mother has been good to me, drawing out my hidden fears in the early years of our marriage. I love the way she persists in naming things – no subjects are taboo, the naming of ills lancing their power to harm, she reckons. And there's that curious thing she has about names themselves. Daniel equals wax in the ears, was the first example she gave me. She swore it had nothing to do with any particular Daniel's character, nor with the sound of the word itself – there are no rational explanations, no conscious associations, she claims. 'Alastair is rather nice,' she told me at Sunday breakfast, my first weekend at Godstow, 'Alastair is a mountain stream in summer. On quite a high mountain. In the Andes. With snow on the summit.' She has never been caught out, the image of a name always the same, all Alastairs over the years remaining streams; given not remembered images, the details sometimes rendered fully sometimes not, their essences unchanging.

She rang me last week, out of the blue. She'd heard on the radio, a moment before, something so ridiculous that she had to tell someone. So telephoned me. President Reagan justifies his fitness for office by the fact that he can pull on his socks while standing up, without resting his foot on a chair! Can you credit it? Your mother is nowhere near as conservative, big 'C' or little, as she looks. I like her. I liked her even when she made me feel I was on parade, the meet-my-famous-son-in-law bit performance. All her friends are the 'best', the 'tops', the 'nicest', aren't they? I like it that your mother eats every scrap of apple except the stalk.

With you lot holidays begin weeks before the day of departure. That time we went to Catalonia I could hardly believe my eyes when you dressed up in a fake flamenco skirt and cooked paella for supper. Get us in the mood, you said. You made it possible for me to treat myself to a needle-striped cotton jacket I'd coveted for years but the good taste of which I'd never trusted on my own. The same trip to town you bought me a blue silk scarf, knotted twice around my neck so frequently it tore, eventually, in two.

Holiday rituals: I loved the creation of our own holiday ritual. Our calling a taxi to drop us off at Tower Hill Underground and save the dispiriting drag of suitcases down the High Street to the station. *London Bridge is falling down, falling down, falling down*: you used to sing as we crossed beneath the toy-town turrets. *My fair lady*: I used to chorus.

Morocco was different. In the taxi on the way to Agadir you cried. I'm crying at my typewriter now. Didn't then. If I'd cried then maybe my trust in us need never have been tested, and none of this would have happened. What we don't do matters as much as what we do, I see.

I packed ice around my heart, to freeze your tears. Succeeded in convincing myself your injury was nothing serious, that the letter business was aggravated by the old unresolved problem: your work, and your doubts as to whether there's any point in weaving, however good at it you might struggle to become.

Become? You're already the best ikat weaver in England, my love.

Stop work for a bit and have a baby: I probably should have said.

'Why do it if you don't want to? No one's forcing you,' I was reduced instead to snapping when your doubts dragged me down.

You cried not sang on our holiday taxi-ride, and I pretended I felt all right. No, I'm fine thanks, I kept telling you. Don't worry about me. It's you who's hurt. Concentrate on yourself.

If I'd admitted then, for a second, the depth of my own pain I'd have. . . I don't quite know what I would have done. Gone crazy?

In the train to Gatwick you criticised me for never reading without a purpose. Why is it you're unable to tolerate my feeling differently to you about anything, even about the books I take on holiday? It's the repetitiveness (apart from the stupidity) of your arguments which annoys me. I've told you, endlessly, how much I enjoy reading up on environmental matters when I'm on holiday. It gives me a sense of security to be on top of the current literature; of comfort from time gainfully employed; of confidence in my expertise. What's wrong with that?

It wasn't too bad once we were there. Heat helps. The sun's heat flattening our bodies to the ground, ironing out the bumps and blemishes, steaming off anxiety. You adore the sun, your oily skin tanning in no time. We both look well in the sun.

Making love comes easier in the heat too. Odd how we've never talked about sex. Perhaps it was me, my customary closing up. DANGER! UNEXPLODED BOMBS! the sign read – and you, obedient you, took note and kept away. Sex never mattered as much to me as it did to you. And don't imagine I didn't realise how often I disappointed you. Don't imagine I didn't feel your breath in bed on the back of my neck, didn't smell your lust. I did my best . . . Funnily enough, our holiday in Agadir worked well on the physical side. I don't recall once failing you. Although failing isn't quite the word. It's more a question of want, of need. I seldom want you when you want me: in that sense a failure.

We're innocents, a couple of novices when it comes to sex. You only took up with me at Oxford through boredom with the meadow fumblings of undergraduates, convinced that a grown working man would have the experience to satisfy you. The romance of the *Oxford Mail*, of my being a journalist also appealed to you, gave you status at art school.

Body as well as heart and head: that's what love should be. I fell in love with you because I needed you to love me, because I decided that to be loved by you would solve all my problems. For life. I nearly gave up – you know that. It was only when I stopped pursuing you, told myself that if you were determined not to have me then I'd better get on as best I could on my own, that you changed your mind. It was you who did the chasing in the end, I who made the decision to love you again, and to take your hand in marriage. With me it all started in the head; though you've come by now to fill my heart as well. Not my body. My body has never loved your body, not like it must be possible to do. I think your body is beautiful, in its way, but I don't love it. I love your face. I adore your face, with its button nose, freckles on the bridge. The symmetry of your features is truly lovely.

When you're naked everything seems to change, even your face changes. It happens. I don't know how.

It's not just that we avoided discussing our sexual dissatisfactions, we never talked about sex at all. I never told you – for example – about the Moroccan boys pestering me on the beach in Agadir. Not the boys selling beads, or rides on their fathers' camels; but the ones flogging their bodies in the dunes. On the morning I trekked up the beach to the flamingo sanctuary I was almost waylaid. Won't tell you how they propositioned me. Too disgusting.

We never noticed how many queers were staying in the hotel. I didn't anyway. If you did you might have mentioned it and then I could have alluded to the 'alternative attractions' in my article, instead of banging on about the ruined fort on the point ('Younger than Hollywood', some wag wrote in to the editor.)

You must admit we're very different. I mean, I wouldn't have dreamt of joining the hotel exercise classes on the beach, run by that jolly Egyptian, fluent in the games-showese of three continents. You're gregarious; me, I'd rather read a book. You participate in everything, make friends everywhere. You wanted me to waste every night with you in the hotel nightclub, shouting at strangers above the din, my forced smile flashing green and red. I can't take the pace any longer, I've run out of steam. Or maybe it's you who've tired? Are you tired, my love, of bearing the enthusiasm for two? I used to love dancing with you. Yards apart – twisting and jiving: *The stomp the bomp the mashed pota-ato too. Any ole dance that you wa-anna do. But le-et's dance* – or pressed heart to heart we used to move as one. Once, at a ball in Pangbourne, we literally swept the floor with our quickstep. Old ladies, puffed powder drifting in the furrows of their cleavage, queued to pay respect. 'Such happiness. Bless you. I was afraid young people had forgotten how to be in love,' one of them said. Remember?

On the dance floor at Ali Baba's we clung to each other like ship-wrecked sailors.

It's because you're different that I married you; so your differentness could rub off on me. My shyness was to become your confidence; my orderedness your spontaneity; my frowns your smiles.

You can bargain, I can't. At the souk in Agadir it was magnificent the way you wheedled that tribal fragment from the old Arab, explaining – in your schoolgirl French – how you're a weaver too. Pretending to leave, drinking coffee, switching the attack to a brass pot you didn't want. The Arab enjoyed himself as well. That's what's special about the way you do things: you get what you want without making anyone else feel bad about it. Quite the opposite in fact: everyone is usually delighted with you. 'Next time, Madame, you buy something. Because I give you this,' the man said at the door of his booth, rustling the spoiled dunam notes in long fingers, nails curved and yellow. 'A quotation from *The Captain of Köpenick*, when Scofield finally buys the uniform,' I pointed out to you. 'The old Moslem's rhetoric repeats Büchner's Jewish tailor's. They're incredibly cultivated, some of these Arabs.'

I felt an idiot typing the fair copy of my long explanatory letter, with you lying behind me on our hotel bed. So unnecessary, this insistence of mine on explaining my unsent letter to Kathy with a hand-delivered monster to you. Why didn't we simply talk about it as you suggested? I must have appeared cold and disconnected – not how I felt at all. And yet, another part of me, the tougher part, wanted it all written down in black and white, so what had happened, the new way I felt, could never be denied. I was more frightened of our us persuading me to turn aside from change than I was of the sadness and uncertainty change itself might bring. I was less anxious about hurting you, my Woolly, than I was of losing Kathy. I couldn't tell you this. I can never tell you this direct and have sought instead to inscribe it between the lines of all my letters, to lay it across the path at the dead-end of every telephone call.

It was a sadly inadequate apology, a banal hymn to my own self-concern and blind misuse of you. Pompous, impotent claptrap.

In all the words that follow, as indeed in life itself, you must remember I always love and cherish you, always care and always share. We will sustain each other all our life whatever happens.

Arrant rubbish!

I am comforted by the knowledge that none of this is wilful, nothing planned, nothing thought of. If I did not trust the deep truth of the need, did not trust the reality of the feelings, I would never forgive myself for this anguish caused us both, you particularly.

Could I possibly have written that? Could I? And did I give it to you?

I was comforted. What about *you* for Christ's sake?

To be more and more myself and less and less concerned about myself was one of my declared intentions. I must have been off my head.

I took your reply – scribbled spontaneously by the pool – away with me up the beach and sat, sobbing, at the edge of the dunes. Boldly, distinctively you stated things as they really were. *Our 'us' is everlasting, but the physical us of you and me may not be*; you wrote. You quoted Donne – the bit about the bond of love being like a pair of compasses, the stronger the pivotal connection the wider the circle of life therein contained – and told me how Persig, hero of your book of the moment, *Zen and the Art of Motorcycle Maintenance*, spoke of quality, the kind of quality you have always seen in me and which you believe is present in every single thing we've done together.

I know I love you your letter concluded, the know underlined three times. *I love you so deeply and completely. Your Woolly.*

Kathy was with me in Agadir – especially in the early mornings, when I felt her presence at my work-table in the hotel's deserted café on the sands: tide out, the beach as yet the preserve of locals scavenging for the night life leftovers of careless tourists; camels bivouacked in groups on the sand, smoke from their drivers' fires rising into the morning air; fishermen waist-deep in the surf, hauling nets of leaping sprats, fuel for thousands of lunchtime *fritures*; exotic birds – exotic to my European eye – guzzling in the damp sand released by the sea's retreat. I would stroll up the beach at each step twisting the ball of my foot and clawing with my toes the soft sand sucked away to meet the incoming wave. My fingers tingled to Kathy's imagined touch. 'Look,' she might have said, stooping to pick up a shell and dropping it into my satchel. My fist clenched to the contrary image, of her wandering down the beach at Harlech in search of shelter from the Irish Sea breeze, hand in hand with somebody else.

No, I'd know if she had a special friend, I remember thinking. ('Wish we were still by the sea. It's been such a lovely day. I don't want it to end,' she more-or-less said when I delivered her back at Roxeth House after the trip to Brighton.)

I longed to see her on my return, and rang to leave a message at Roxeth House within minutes of getting into work. Afterwards, every time the phone went I hoped it would be her, each upward tilted 'Hello?' pitched at Kathy. Once it was you – and you noticed my disappointment. I know you did. I had to telephone again the following day before Kathy returned my call, and agreed to come for a walk with me in Richmond Park, in the late afternoon of her next day off.

In the car on our drive across town I struggled for things sensibly to say, something which had never happened before in conversation with Kathy. Till then with Kathy the words had come easily, I'd been fluent – poetic even – about ideas and feelings I did not know I had. To bridge the silence I told her about your cultivated Arab in the souk. Guess what she said, with more than a hint of ridicule in her voice? 'Sounds most unlikely. Probably the other way round.' By which she meant that instead of the Arab having read Büchner it was likely to be a standard bazaari phrase which the playwright had heard somewhere else and included, out of context, in his script.

We never thought of that, did we?

She comes out with comments like that all the time. Honestly, I never knew a Kathy Abraham woman existed. I didn't. I never imagined meeting a woman who could challenge me to think and say exactly what I mean, about everything. I don't know how she dares to. She does though, and through her I challenge too. Kathy's openness, her truthfulness is different from yours and your mother's. I know you and your mother talk together unembarrassedly, about almost anything – like when the two of you hooted with laughter in telling me how you used to piss standing up; used to stop scooting down the street and piss in your pants, standing up. Kathy, you see, would want to know why, whereas you and your mother laugh such things off and bash on confidently to the next event. Kathy considers it essential to understand what's happening, to assess what she feels at any one time before moving forward.

Kathy is from a different generation, spared our repression. We were teenagers in the Sixties and yet neither of us slept around, took drugs or played in a group. I never went to a single pop concert.

How can I hope to exist in the Eighties when I funked the Sixties?

With Kathy's help I might. She hasn't compromised,

that's what I find inspiring. She reminds me of possibilities for myself I long ago rejected. With her I surprise myself.

With you I'm not properly me, I'm an offspring, a satellite of us.

Of you.

I don't think you realise how possessive you are of people. You won't let any of us fly free, will you? Look how you keep Barry Macdonald permanently attached – like a kite – giving a periodic tug to the string so he knows you're there, occasionally hauling him all the way in. That ridiculous fluffy hippopotamus he gave you on your eighteenth birthday, why do you keep it, upside down on a shelf in your wardrobe?

I should have made you throw it out years ago.

It's sweet: you used to say. Looks like Barry.

It's ugly: I should have replied. An ugly symbol of your possessiveness.

Kathy finds our use of a joint nickname sinister. She says it displays an unhealthy desire for loss of self, an evasion of autonomous responsibility. She's got it wrong, of course. Too young – too clever, too? – to appreciate the wonder of love.

We do, my Woolly, we do.

'Woolly': your half-humorous half-serious image of babies arriving ready-wrapped in wool, like lambs.

I parked the car at the top of Richmond Hill, with a view out over terraced gardens and the mansard roof of the Star and Garter to wide sweeps of the Thames. Kathy and I walked in through the iron gates, across the inner road and down the side of a small plantation towards the nearest stretch of heathland. I slowed once we'd cleared the family groups of would-be footballers, frisbee freaks and reluctant fathers playing hide-and-seek, and Kathy took her place at my side. I laid a hand for an instant in the small of her back.

'I thought about you a lot in Agadir,' I said.

She kind-of-laughed, not shyly as I'd imagined she might, but harshly. 'I hardly think of you at all when I'm not with you.'

'No reason why you should,' I said.

'I know there isn't.'

My stomach went tight; I walked on in silence, head bent to the ground.

'What thoughts did you have of me?' she asked.

'About work, and things . . .' I didn't finish my sentence. I would have done, with a word of encouragement.

'Look Alastair.' Kathy had stopped and was staring me full in the face. 'You'd better tell me what you feel about me. It's not right the way you half say things and expect people to understand. Tell me straight.'

'It's complicated. I'm not always sure what I feel . . .'

'Go on.'

'I can't. Are you always certain?'

Kathy grimaced. 'Yes I am,' she said. 'It's the only thing one can ever hope to know, everything else is a matter of opinion. I may not like my feelings, may not always know what to do about them, how to react. But at least I know what they are. And so do you, if you're honest with yourself.'

We walked on down a grassy track between parched bracken. I felt easier with Kathy in the lead, my gaze fixed to the waves of black hair bouncing on the shoulders of her blouse, edged in red.

I began to tell her. 'With you I feel I'm getting somewhere. Moving on. Through meeting you my perception of many things has changed. Like . . .'

I held back, wary of the thought which had entered my head: concerning Kathy's Anglo-Jewishness and the whole sordid story of British anti-semitism. Until meeting her, I was on the point of saying, and reading Primo Levi's insufferably sad book – which she left me beneath the Roxeth House Christmas tree – I had had only the shadiest idea of the Holocaust and what it might be like to be a Jew. (Pathetic, I now see, but true at the time.)

Once settled on this tack I would probably have gone on to tell her about my long vac as a summer camp counsellor in upstate New York, teaching spoilt Jewish kids from Yonkers to sail. I might well have admitted to Kathy that even after a whole summer of sabbath shalöms and geffilte fish, in my arrogant Englishness it still hadn't occurred to me to wonder how six million Jews had been exterminated within reach of every adult I know – of every teacher, all my university lecturers, my uncles and aunts, my mother and my father – and that not one of them had expressed to me their horror at what they allowed to happen. If pushed I would also have confessed my then-recent awareness of a shameful mistake. Would have told her of the insulting way I ignored the attempts of that summer's love – Ruth, a counsellor at Cally Bay's sister camp on the other side of the lake: I must have told you about her – to dissuade me from visiting her at home in Ohio on, I now realise, Yom Kippur. Instead of describing to Kathy the darkened silent house; instead of telling her of my insistence on having something to eat; instead of . . . instead of daring to reveal my weakness I went on:

'You're a bit like a friend I had at school. In your help with my writing. And in your forcing me to think properly. My friend – Colin Simpson – used to get all the top novels sent to him in school the moment they came out. He used to lend them to me. *Clockwork Orange* I must have read when I was fourteen. Colin was a brilliant writer. I often think he should be me. I mean . . .'

Kathy turned to me, smilingly.

'Yes'.

'Colin's dead. He killed himself. Blew off his head with his father's shotgun. Not at school. A couple of years ago. I never knew he was in trouble. He went up to Cambridge, and I never kept in touch.'

Kathy dropped back into step at my side, and touched my elbow with the tips of her fingers. 'You do make me laugh sometimes,' she said. 'You still haven't told me. Have you?'

'Haven't I? Being with you means a lot to me.'

'And what do you think it means to me?'

'The same,' I blurted out.

'Fair enough.'

That's what she said. She did. Just loud enough to hear. I promise you she did.

We were walking in time, Kathy's long strides easily keeping pace with mine. Her height, almost as tall as me: I like that.

'And your holiday? Why wasn't it fun?' she asked.

'Because Dinah and I are having problems.'

'Think I hadn't noticed? I'm not an imbecile.'

I wanted to bury my head in her hair – although I was nowhere near actually doing it. And I didn't tell her any details about us. Told her it had nothing to do with her, that it needn't involve her at all.

'But it *does* involve me. It must,' she insisted. 'There's no point in friendship if we can't share the important things. The Appeal, books and ideas, they're nothing. If we can't talk about personal things, what's the use?'

I didn't know what to say, taken aback by the emotion in her voice. I mumbled something about hating her to get caught up in the mess.

'You reckon you can be all things to all people,' she said, a little further on. 'Sociable and gay for Dinah. Trendy intellectual to the media lot. Serious with me. Which of them is you?'

You've never asked me that. It's never occurred to you that I might be putting on an act, has it? If we'd ever had a conversation like that things wouldn't be in such a muddle. How is it I didn't tell *you* about Colin Simpson? How is it *you* haven't taken the trouble to discover something so central to me? I've felt guilty for years about Colin. About the way he looked up to me for my success at school. Especially for the sailing. You should have seen how proud he was of me, how happy he was when I won the All England Schools Trophy. And I lacked the common grace to return the compliment and make him understand how fantastic I thought he was, how much more significant his achievements were: his writing and languages, and the rest. Colin won the essay prize every year. Every single year. Colin committed suicide and I, his best friend, had never noticed his depressions.

Now I'm the writer, the 'famous' campaigning journalist. He's dead and I – who had to get my mother to write my Prep School compositions; who, aged seventeen, in the final of the reading competition, sight-read suffragettes (Dickens: *Pickwick Papers*) as if it was an exclamation, with a hard 'g': 'Suffragettes!' – I am alive and writing.

There was more I wanted from Kathy, and on returning to the car I proposed a drink in a nearby pub.

She ordered a gin-and-orange. (Unexpected. She's always doing the unexpected.)

'You never enquire about my private life, do you?' she said when I sat down beside her with our drinks.

'I suppose not.'

'You should. Might learn something.'

'Like what?'

'That I've got a relationship.'

'Several I presume. With me for one.'

'No, I'll never have a relationship with you. Besides, I'm faithful to Alan.'

I hadn't immediately understood what she meant by 'relationship'. Was a bit shocked, I expect.

'You don't seem to see much of each other,' I eventually responded.

'We don't choose to.'

'But you want to marry him one day?'

Kathy twisted her glass round and round on the pub table. 'No,' she replied, 'He's not that special.'

That's what she said. I remember every word. She could have ended it then if she'd wanted to. If she'd felt like smothering my young-love for her – which I *know* she knew about – she could have done so then. But she didn't. She had her chance and she chose not to take it. What was I to think? How do you expect me to have felt?

Kathy does nothing casually: you can rely on that.

What's more I could smell perfume. While I was getting the drinks she must have dabbed some perfume behind her ears.

What was that meant to mean, tell me that? You're a woman, you should know.

Kathy Abraham was aware of her reputation for altruism – being distant from the truth it quite amused her. She was interested in people, liked people on the whole, and had set out to help the residents of Roxeth House in ways they themselves most wanted; but in no part did she claim a mission to serve. If she managed to be loved by the old women at the Nursing Home more than any other trainee, this Kathy put down to her ability to think, not to a presumed vocation. She did not feel sorry for her patients' plight. Sympathy, she had long ago observed, lay dangerously close to pity. Kathy was interested in all people, in ill people no differently from well people, and this, she felt, was the correct approach to her first serious job.

Alastair intrigued Kathy. Although physically not at all her type, she nevertheless found him distinctly attractive; she could not work him out, and this drew her. Short strong-armed men had never previously appealed – the less so if they smoked. A showy smoker of French cigarettes, Alastair carried on conversations with a Gitane *bout filtré* lodged at the corner of his mouth, large blue eyes screwed half-shut against the smoke, a habit Kathy intensely disliked. At least he kept his fingers free of nicotine stains, she later noticed – noticing, in the same moment, his hands: reliable hands with muscular drumstick thumbs and prominent veins, his fingernails cut short. Another, weightier criticism which Kathy levelled at Alastair in those early days was his tendency to talk down to people, to treat women – the Home was staffed entirely by women, as well as being exclusively for their use – as if, by definition, they needed to be told things not asked. Although this again was a fault Kathy later found herself forgiving. It was not arrogance or self-certainty which led him to behave like this, she discovered, but impatience. An impatience to get things done. There was, she began to appreciate, a touching reticence – the opposite of arrogance – in his manner. In his sideways stance in conversation, darting gaze averted; in the half-hidden questioning appeal of his eyebrow frown; in the impression he gave, when he took the time to listen, of valuing the opinion of the maddest resident no less highly than his own.

All the same, in Kathy's probationary months at Roxeth House she was friendlier with Dinah than with Alastair.

Dinah used to call round to Roxeth House twice a week with Fifi Vollmer to help out at lunch, their presence a welcome diversion in the patients' routine, inducing – Kathy catalogued – a forgetfulness of food fads. Kathy liked Dinah's indelible good humour, all the jokes and jollity and generosity. She admired the way Dinah expended more energy in a single lunch-hour than she had given of herself to anything in her whole life – or to anybody, for that matter.

Kathy was surprised when Alastair asked her to lend a hand with the Appeal, for at the time he seemed barely aware of her existence. His summary of the Appeal's aims and of the responsibilities he required her to assume was so gruffly, so unclearly put that Kathy quizzed Dinah about it later in the week. Dinah encouraged her, told her how bright Alastair considered her to be. Dinah explained that Alastair was dreadfully over worked, with another *British City* TV series to write, on top of his weekly column and that her helping out with the Appeal would be 'simply marvellous'. Matron, it transpired, had already altered the roster to free her for five hours a week on the Home's Appeal, leaving her no choice. Tempted to object to the assumption of her acquiescence she admitted, instead, to feeling flattered. It meant she was to be taken seriously by people much older than herself, people who already counted. It made her feel grown-up, adult, the formation of this intimate working relationship with a man old enough to be her uncle; a man whose wife so trusted him – and herself – that jealousy could be forgotten. Kathy feared jealousy. To be jealous was to lose everything: pride, dignity, grace, judgement, sensitivity, equanimity. Kathy was determined never to envy anyone anything.

The more she saw of Alastair the less she found to criticise. Judged by outward appearances he seemed suited to the kind of media success ambitious hard work had earned him and yet, beneath the fashionable haircut and Italian flannel trousers, the Boston sneakers and monogrammed Hong Kong shirts lurked, Kathy became convinced, a man to whom all of this meant very little; a man to whom it was a convenient disguise, a shell within which the real Alastair-snail lay juicily concealed. His taste intrigued her. There were many things Kathy could see he enjoyed about his work: not least its being talked about, the intended effect of the provocative line he took on familiar subjects and of the architectural prominence his articles accorded areas of London others ignored. Kathy liked this in Alastair. Liked the disrespect it implied for standard goals and rewards – his determination to do things well not because the end-result was necessarily worth the effort but because the doing was. This coincided with how Kathy felt about her work at Roxeth House, undertaken principally for negative reasons – because she had been unable to think of any reason not to – but which she was no less committed to doing well than she might have been to something closer to her heart.

On their trip to Brighton Kathy learnt how, at school, the notion of conventional success had come to mean nothing to Alastair, this and other confidences raising in her feelings of a complex intensity, for she knew – instinctively – that Alastair had shared certain thoughts with no one else, definitely not with Dinah and possibly not even with himself. It seemed to Kathy, on thinking about it, to be the truth. She had no difficulty visualising Alastair as a busy teenager, eager to please, programmed to be top at everything. She admired the way he refused to blame others for the disappointment of not being made Head of School, an honour which everyone – masters, senior boys in front of him, his father (especially his father, Acting Assistant Chief Planner of North Yorkshire) – had led him to view as his by right. There had been no coercion, he had assured Kathy when she pressed for explanations. He had enjoyed himself at the time, he said; no serious alternative had occurred to him – except to be bad, at which he had never been any good, he told her. Only at the end, when the crowning glory eluded him, had Alastair regretted his mistaken expectations. Stupid, and ungrateful: his disappointed father had railed when he turned down a place at Magdalen, Oxford to read PPE, in favour of Eng Lit at Durham.

The better Kathy came to know Alastair the more securely she was convinced it would be an error to have sex with him – although there were times when she was tempted: not because she fancied him, but because he clearly fancied her, and his daring to do so little about it annoyed her. The twinkle in his eye, charming at the outset, she turned against, suspecting it hid the kind of attitude to intimacy she abhorred. Serve him right if we do end up in bed: she threatened, beneath her breath. Then he really would be confused!

Yet Kathy was herself somewhat confused by her own feelings for Alastair. For there were other times – times when he talked about architecture, shared with her his love for particular buildings, particular city spaces – when she could not help but admire him, sensing his weight and substance. Her friendship with Alastair began to have a detrimental effect on Kathy's contact with Alan, a boy she knew from university and had recently started a relationship with. Alan was on occasion reduced, in Kathy's vision, to a shadow in the light of Alastair. The way Alan worked solely when he needed money, and then only at some worthless task – telephone salesman of cosmetic accessories, or peak hour National Car Park attendant – no longer always appealed to Kathy. Occasionally repelled.

Ironically, Kathy liked Alan best when he did not have a job at all and spent his days, every day, weekends too, constructing model steam locomotives in the big basement room he rented in a carpet store in Camberwell. Whenever she felt like seeing him, there she could guarantee he would be: painting the appropriate livery on some rolling stock or casting, in his miniature forge, the steel flywheels of a new engine.

Kathy had her own key. 'Hi Kath. Won't be a moment,' he would say.

Kathy adored Alan's loving of her body and his not caring in the least about the rest. She adored the way he took off her clothes differently every time, paying unequal disordered attention to different parts of her anatomy as the mood struck. Kathy refused to say she loved Alan, admitted merely to liking him – very much. She very much liked the security of knowing he would always take care of himself, and leave her to look after herself. She treasured this freedom from the usual obligation to indulge man's need to feel needed. Kathy felt free with Alan, free to let herself be pleasured as she pleased, without having to satisfy him in return. Kathy and Alan laughed a lot whilst making love, constantly surprising each other with the shapes their bodies made, the fitting together in unexpectedly sensuous configurations.

There was only one rule which Kathy made, secretly to herself, with regard to Alan: that each touch, each coming together, was to be satisfying in itself, for her at that moment. Everything she did, or allowed to be done to her, was for the moment. When she ran her hand over the smooth skin of his penis, stroked him with her tongue, felt his sperm on her face, in her throat, she did all this for herself not for him. To feel precisely how his penis worked. To gauge its size and strength, and test its reaction to a subtleness of touch unfelt, by her, when buried inside. To relish her own power, knowing how easy it would be for her teeth to hurt. Knowing he knew this too.

Another nice thing about Alan was his indifference to the concept of an ideal woman. It never entered Alan's head that Kathy should, or could, be anybody but herself. Not like most men. Most men, as far as Kathy could make out, lived in tinted expectation of finding a woman to match their ideal image: of Tina Turner, Isabelle Huppert, Princess Di, or the Rossellini girl, depending on personal twists of taste. Kathy hated this about men. Hated it because it cheated life, made life a game, a charade.

Alan possessed integrity: in everything he did and said Alan was true to himself. Alastair, she suspected, told himself the truth only in his dreams. To act with integrity did not mean things would necessarily come right, but without integrity everything – Kathy believed – was bound to turn out wrong.

Trust was another of the concerns which fuelled Kathy's youthful passion. 'I trust you. I trust you completely,' a boy she once thought she loved had said to her. At the time she had taken this as a compliment, a mark of respect; though she now realised it was no such thing. When a man told a woman he trusted her he was not honouring, he was burdening her. 'I depend on you to protect me from hurt,' he was actually saying. 'Now that I've placed my trust in you you must never let me down, you must forever be the person I need and expect you to be.' Burden someone with trust and they are locked for life into the unchanging image of some once-glimpsed dream. Most marriages existed in the image of what people thought they ought to be, not how they were. There seemed no escaping the treadmill, each generation repeating in reverse the errors of the last, no two persons ever able to secure a balance: between love and ambition (of parents for their child); between respect and rebellion (of child against parent); between letting go and holding on (husband to wife, wife to husband, lover to lover).

Kathy's greatest fear – greater than her fear of jealousy – was that one day she might be reduced to pinning her hopes of fulfilment on the succeeding generation, on her own children – or on another's should she bear none. Sensing the same fear in Alastair, she brushed aside his faults and admired instead his self-possessedness. 'Why is it you like me?' she had asked him on their day away together. 'Because I like myself. Mostly. More often than not, anyway. When I'm with you,' he had replied. Kathy forgave Alastair a lot for that reply. Forgave him when his involvement with self deteriorated into an obsession. On his birthday, for example, back in March. When he turned up unexpectedly at Roxeth House and persuaded her to take her lunchbreak with him on the heath, the picnic pre-prepared in a wicker hamper: a bottle of wine (and Perrier), glasses, napkins, delicious club sandwiches, fresh fruit and gooey eclairs. Sitting on a bench in the spring sun Alastair had taken everything she said she thought and said she did as if it related to him, as if she was incapable of action on her own account. Even this silly assumption of reactive dependence on him she was prepared to overlook. The one thing Kathy could never forgive, however, would never tolerate, was the possibility that Alastair might become dependent on her.

It had happened before. Several times. The cloying, sighing, belittling, imprisoning dependence of so-called man's so-called love. Kathy loathed the havoc this 'love' wreaked on people's lives, loathed herself for allowing it to happen, for not spotting the signs earlier and pulling out. Kathy knew by then that foolishness in love was the norm not the exception. She expected it now, and looked in the men she met – like Alan; and Alastair, she reckoned – for proof of their being different before risking friendship. Kathy's experiences had led her to accept, finally, that her father's devastation at her mother's death was not the ugly inhuman aberration it had seemed to her at the time, but how most men behaved.

All the same, she could never forget. Kathy could never forget the transformation before her barely teenage eyes of a creative, confident husband – her father – into a snivelling child. A widower. It frightened her still, for she could make no sense of it. Her mother had been ill for years, death an ever present threat, their flat in Hammersmith a cool dark haven for her mother's frailty. Kathy's Aunt Hilda, who stayed on after the funeral, attempted to cheer the place up – whilst her father religiously reinstated every altered photograph, removed each vase of cut flowers, lowered the raised blinds. A week after Aunt Hilda left Kathy returned home from school one afternoon to find her father standing in the hall of their mansion flat holding out her mother's cardigan. She put it on. The next day it was a dress. Then shoes . . . then, in the end, the hair. Every evening when he returned from work Kathy's father made her tie up her hair exactly like her mother's. He never tried to touch her, nor make her touch him, was content to watch his daughter do her homework at the dining room table dressed as his dead wife. Two hours an evening for five years, five evenings a week, Kathy Abraham changed into her mother's clothes to please her father. Until she left home to take up her place at university; and her father passed his evenings in the pub on the Mall instead – where he met and married another woman, fat and friendly, the opposite of Kathy's mother.

Love, Kathy had subsequently worked out, went wrong when it was made exclusive. Everyone needed love. Not a single soul-love but all sorts of loves and lovings. Different things from different people – often at the same time. In the old days commitment for life was terminated by the death of one partner or the other within a decade, two at the most. But life these days could literally mean a life's sentence: fifty years or more. How could two people find exclusive satisfaction one in the other for fifty years? It was ridiculous; Kathy argued with her friends. Not that she advocated concealed, hermetic love instead. Not at all. Kathy's loves were to live openly, lover alongside lover, the central commitment making way from time to time for secondary involvements. Kathy envisaged meeting at some undisclosed date in the future a man she would never marry but whose children she would bear. She would love this man in changing ways all her life. Their love, their commitment would be a central feature of both their lives – not the only commitment, though. Kathy planned a non-exclusive central love which would permit secondary loves to come and go in orbit around her alone, not them the couple.

Kathy despised the ideal of coupledom: because it negated an individual woman's right to a life of her own. All women, in Kathy's scheme of things, had a right to emotional and sexual experiment at their own pace in their own time, regardless of the needs of men. One of the saddest moments in Kathy Abraham's young life was the discovery that Miss Gaydon, at sixty-two years old, a girls' games teacher all her working days, did not know how to masturbate. Miss Gaydon's sexual development had been so blighted by the ideal, unfulfilled in her, of coupledom that she had never learnt to pleasure herself. Society, Kathy concluded, had got love wrong.

Getting love right mattered more to Kathy than anything else in the world.

You think that when I came up to stay with you in Glasgow I'd already decided. You think I orchestrated the whole thing to suit myself. You say I never took the slightest notice of how you felt, of what you wanted us to do. You say that my declarations of love were a matter merely of habit. Puke, you actually said. Dried puke.

I hadn't made up my mind before that awful weekend, as a matter of fact; and nor did I afterwards, on the way home in the train. I can't remember ever deciding anything, if you want to know the truth.

I still can't see the point of educated people living like savages, as the Challises do. On both sides of every step of the staircase, on all three floors, there's rubbish: dirty clothes (not only the children's), pieces of toy, half-eaten bowls of cereal, books, papers, tissues, letters, telephone directories, cheque stubs, football boots, cigarettes, coins, music, dog biscuits . . . It's plain selfish bringing children up in a pigsty, not liberating at all (anti-pedagogic: Challis calls it). And you admire the man?

It fitted your frame of mind, PG-ing for two months in that manic household. Martin Challis' insidious influence has a lot to answer for. He gave you the part-term lectureship place didn't he? No, perhaps he wasn't Head of Faculty then. What did he want from you?

Late night bouts of conversation at the Challises' kitchen table: a child dispatched from in front of the television to fetch himself, his parents and whoever else was there a selection of lukewarm cartons from the Chinese takeaway; Carol's playscript pushed to one end of the table where its crinkled edges absorbed spilt coffee, empty beer cans stacked on top; guru Martin leading his gang a jig through the banana groves of left wing culture . . . I can't bear how understanding those types are, the way they're so bloody tolerant – notably of their enemies' *in*tolerance. Christ, if I held their views about society I'd be permanently up in arms fighting injustice. What merit is there in passive benevolence? You say he's wonderful with the students. You say it's fantastic how he encourages each group of students to build an individual framework within which to conduct their own chosen process of learning. Enablement: that's your new key-word, stolen from Challis.

And how do you think you'd have become such a skilful weaver if nobody had taught you, may I ask? Chat never got anyone anywhere. Martin's armchair activism – one arm broken – is no better than the Blue Rinse sets in Bognor, the arms of their chairs protected by lace doilies. Charles Rennie Mackintosh, in whose masterpiece Challis promulgates his weedy seed, drank himself to death in the Dordogne rather than tolerate the high-art crap of the educated élite, the soft-spoken low-church selfism of Glasgow's rich. I'm glad, I tell you, I'm a journalist. Who earned us a living? Who kept your studio warm? Who paid for your mistakes? I did – and not by staying up half the night spouting rubbish.

Now you have the nerve to say I'll never be a writer. That I don't have the heart to be a real writer.

What I do every week, *that's* real writing. Because it's read by real people.

I'm sorry.

I don't mean to sound critical. I'm not. I love your openness to outside influences. I do. I always have, you know I have. I love your buoyancy. Your mother tells everyone your first spoken phrase was 'good idea.' Whenever you were asked a question you used to wrinkle your nose in mimicked thought and reply, 'good idea.' 'Would you like an icecream, Dinah?' 'Good idea.' 'Want to do khaki?' 'Good idea.'

I can see you saying it, my Woolly.

Sarah-Jane and I never said anything unusual as children. I was so well-behaved at parties other mothers used to ask if I felt sick. Sing-songs were the best thing that happened to me as a child – on long journeys, bouncing up and down on the back seat of the Humber (except on steep hills, when Sarah-Jane and me held our breath: so the radiator wouldn't boil over).

I'm not suggesting you didn't make me happy, most of the time.

In Glasgow, though, we didn't think it possible to be more miserable. Such blackness, when for nine married years all we'd known was light: all around us, inside and out. In the big park down the road from the Challises' we discovered utter devastation, the grass bared to brown earth, ravaged by dogs and children. One end of the boating lake was used as a tip, full of junk dumped from car boots; supermarket trollies loaded with DIY debris and rolled down the bank to lie half-submerged in the water. I felt so cold on our walks round and round that park. Talking. Talking. Talking. What did we say? What did all those words mean? I've never felt as cold as I did in Glasgow that week. I can't remember it ever being daytime – a mist or smog or something blotted out the days. The nights I remember: two single beds pushed together, the mattresses working themselves apart during the night to reveal in the morning a gaping hole between us. It was so cold in the Challises' spare room we wore pullovers and socks in bed.

Sunday was a nightmare.

I should have let you stay in bed and sleep away your exhaustion. No reason to drag you out into the streets: it's me who can't cope with the Challises, not you. All the local cafés were closed. Hardly any buses running on a Sunday either, and I made you trudge into the city centre for breakfast – in a deserted hotel dining room, with a drunk in a dinner jacket asleep on the floor behind a curtain. Do you remember?

I lied to you when I said I hadn't seen *The Shining*. I had. I'd seen it two days before in the same cinema, one afternoon while you were teaching. It's the only Jack Nicholson film I've thoroughly disliked – but you loved it; and I pretended to too.

I think I'm more ashamed of lying to you about a movie than I am of changing the way I love you.

Glasgow at its best is beautiful. I prefer the dark stone uncleaned, the red bricks blackened by Clydeside soot, defunct dirt a memorial to the vanished industries on which the city is founded. A developer is restoring Miss Cranston's Tea Rooms to their teetotal glory (now that architects are fashionable; especially *Art Nouveau* architects, as Mackintosh is constantly misnomered). Kelvingrove Museum is a jewel: a bloated neo-baroque pearl of a jewel to be sure, set within elaborately enamelled cartouches. It sits, partly hidden, near the edge of a rococo garden, escaping the gothic folly of Gilbert Scott's University buildings on the hill above. A carpet factory dressed as a Turkish bazaar, a war memorial as a . . .

What do I think I'm doing? This is exactly the kind of writing Kathy, quite rightly, says I must eradicate. Not easy. Look at it: bursting out even here. I'm jargon-writing to myself now!

Rejection. You say you first felt the impact of rejection in Glasgow.

I felt rejected by you too, excluded from your Art School world. Waiting. I always seemed to be waiting for you, my eyes averted from the smirky stares of your colleagues – 'See there, that's Alastair Shore. Silly sap.'

You seemed deliberately to cut me out of contact, physically blocked my path through to a world in which I can perfectly well hold my own. You turned an ice-cold shoulder in my face and stopped me participating in anything. In everything. Such a blow. My Dinah, who used to draw me into her conversations, encourage me to take a place warm at her side, my Dinah barred my entry to her circle. It was cruel of you, you realize. There's a vindictive streak in you I used to refuse to see. You take pleasure in punishment – your own too. When you can't get at me you punish yourself, hoping I'll feel guilty. I wish you wouldn't. The damage to me is only skin deep, it quickly heals. The harm you'll do yourself, if you persist, could cripple you.

You were cruel to me in Stockholm as well – years ago, before we were married – excluded me there too. 'You didn't have to come,' you said. 'I never asked you to come,' you said.

It's true. When you won the travel scholarship and elected to be that famous – I've forgotten her name – Swedish weaver's assistant, you made it clear you didn't want me to visit you. And I ignored your rejection. Dinah's wrong. Dinah doesn't understand how rare it is, a love like ours: I told myself. That time I didn't let you shut me out – and you made me suffer for daring to disagree. You made me feel like a damp blanket. I'll never be fun, I tell you. I'll never lead pranks, tell jokes, play pub pianos, dance on tables, jump into fountains with my clothes on. Nor initiate sex – not casually anyway. At school, in my first year at Hillhead, a group of older boys used to trap me in a corner of the 'rears' and force me to listen to dirty jokes until I laughed – or cried: they weren't particular.

I usually cried.

I still don't find dirty jokes fun. I don't find fun fun.

In Stockholm you and four or five of the other foreign students did everything in a group together, meeting up each evening in a favourite café to hatch the night's escapade. A steamer trip up the Baltic coast had been arranged for two of the days of my week's holiday. I was welcome to join you all if I wanted to, it was entirely up to me: you coolly informed me. How do you imagine I felt? After all my letters, my longing for time with you?

You must have intended to hurt. As it did. I felt humiliated.

I'm pleased I stayed behind in Stockholm. I am now, at least – although I can still touch, in my memory, the loneliness of those days. On your return you couldn't resist telling me stories of the fun you'd had dressing up in a sheet as Hamlet's ghost, prancing about the deck half naked.

Give it time, give it time.

I'll strangle the next person who tells me that. 'Give it time, Alastair,' Kathy said when we last met.

How long?

By the time it's right for her it'll be wrong for me. It'll be too late, we'll have missed the moment we could have lost ourselves together, could have given ourselves to love.

I'm ready. She can trust me now.

I'm better now.

Why won't she trust me?

You were the first girl I properly went to bed with – apart from Susannah, sort-of; and Clare Raybould, I keep forgetting her. Did I ever tell you about Lizzie Thomas? She was great, the prettiest girl around in those days: a blonde, really well-developed, and nice with it. She quite liked me in the beginning – until her patience ran out. The Thomases lived in a village six or seven miles from York. I used to cycle over, hide my bike in a ditch and stalk through the fields behind her house to a place where I could spy into the garden. Many afternoons of the school holidays passed that way – summer evenings too, when Mum was at Fellowship meetings. I did it in the snow once, terrified she'd spot me from her bedroom window; keeping extra close beneath the hedges, stopping dead for minutes on end while the birds settled to my presence.

Lizzie and I became friends once I gave up worshipping her. A couple of years later I was due over at Tinbury on Boat Race afternoon. Driving too fast down the country lanes I had to slam on the brakes to avoid hitting a pheasant, and lost control of the car. The car (my father's) took its life into its own hands, tried to climb a bank on the left, rolled over and slid thirty yards down the road on its roof. None of the doors would open and I had to crawl out through the smashed windscreen, upside down, frightened by the drip of petrol. The Thomases' house wasn't far away; I walked up the deserted lane, joined them in the television room and waited till the race was over to tell them what had happened.

Our family car a write-off, and my mother was hardly angry. She's always been like that: terrorised me over minor accidents – breaking a sherry glass, say – and been instantly forgiving about the big things, the real dangers.

When I was a child I felt physically sick with fear at the fortnightly ritual of fingernail cutting, fear not for a slip of the scissors' edge but for its thwack across my knuckles if I'd dared bite a single nail.

At the Challises' I remember watching Carol bite with her teeth her son's toenails when she couldn't find a pair of scissors.

Isn't it amazing how successful that play of hers has been? I never imagined Carol Challis would be a name to drop. She and Yo Yo Ma are the best of my current dinner party who-you-knows. A friend's step-daughter goes to school with Yo-Yo Ma's son in Cambridge, Mass, and she said to me the other day in her soft Bostonian drawl: 'Do you know what Yo Yo Ma means, Alastair? It means Happy-Happy Horse.' With you and your father the stories are always about the family. You tell yourselves the same old tales over and over again, laughing in exactly the same way in exactly the same places. As if anyone else could be interested in the Pollard family sagas? My heart sank to my shoes whenever time your father turned up to bore the dinner table: 'When *was* it, darling? Christopher was still at Wellington. It must've been after Geoffie had mumps, because I'd only just put the rest of us on BUPA . . .' The family is the only topic of conversation your father brightens to. And cricket. And his garden.

It's seldom the expected images, good or bad, which dominate. When something extraordinary happens one says to oneself: 'Wow! That's fantastic! I'll never forget that.' Or at something significant one reads. Or a beautiful view one sees. We usually do forget though, often very quickly. The image of you smiling through your tears on the platform of Glasgow Central Station was one of those things I said I'd never forget; and in this case I haven't, nor ever will. I cried in public, broke down in a railway carriage full of people. I've cried in front of strangers many times since, and don't mind any more. But I did then. The memory of you left behind on the platform, your raised arm pulling the hem of your coat above the knees of your black woollen stockings, will never desert me.

When I got back to London I learnt that Kathy had quit

Roxeth House. No one knew why she left so suddenly, at a day's notice. Packed her bags and walked out.

I couldn't find a note anywhere. Sandra said she dropped in at the office on Friday with her Appeal papers, all perfectly in order, the current position summarised on sheets pinned to the appropriate folder. 'Bye Sandra,' was all she'd said. Matron may have known more – she gave me Kathy's father's address and telephone number. I spoke to her father, who said he'd ask Kathy to ring me. I wrote to her too.

Miss Gaydon went catatonic when Kathy left like that. I don't understand how she could have done it, left them without a word. They had come to rely on her, to trust her, and she walked out on them without a word.

It was a test, a serious test of my faith in her. I had to tell myself over and over again that Kathy must have known what she was up to, that there had to be a perfectly good explanation – if only I could retain my trust in her.

In a way I admire her for it. In a way I'd have been disappointed if she hadn't done it, hadn't shown her strength. Hadn't done something unpredictable. If you're going to do it, do it. Without a fuss. If you've decided to go, go. Go without a backward glance or you'll be turned to stone, to a loveless pillar of salt licked by cows.

Kathy didn't telephone for ten days. At home in the evenings I was constantly lifting up the phone, not to dial her father's number – he didn't know where she was living, he maintained, truthfully as I later found out – but to check there wasn't a fault on the line. I'd put the receiver back down double-quick, worried that at that very moment Kathy might be trying to ring me. I didn't want her to get the wrong impression, to imagine I might be chattering to someone else, unmindful of her.

Neither did I want her to feel pressured by me. In her own time – it could only be any good in her own time, I had already accepted.

Coffee would be best, she said. Not dinner. No, she wouldn't be able to have dinner with me. She'd call round for coffee on Monday morning, at home if that's what I preferred. Yes, she owed me an explanation: she promised.

Waiting. Waiting all weekend. At least I was waiting for something, not nothing. On Monday I would know.

My expectations dipped and soared. From being convinced of her imminent marriage, to being equally certain she'd chucked her boyfriend and decided to do a D Phil: on the culture of privilege, another of her fancied themes. I went for my long walk down the hill to Greenwich, through Brunel's tunnel to the Isle of Dogs, along the Limehouse and Wapping side of the river to Tower Bridge, then back home via the dismal by-ways of New Cross and Deptford. To clear my head. On Sunday I cleaned the house – cleaned the lavatory and bathroom, dusted the rest – opening all the windows to expel the smell of cigarettes. Tomorrow, after you've seen Kathy, then you'll cut down on the Gitanes: I ordered myself. If you can give up smoking Kathy won't get married: I bargained. And the drink? A bottle of wine a night, sometimes two; staggering out into the cold to buy cheap sweet wine from the Indians. It can't have helped. Mind you, I remember thinking how little difference drink made. I remember feeling resilient and strong, and believing this proved I was doing the right thing. If I could drink and smoke as much as I did and still hold my own at work, still stay in control, then I must be on the right road: I used to argue.

At eleven-fifteen she still hadn't arrived.

I made myself not be worried. No use feeling sorry for myself, a weak me was no use to Kathy. Don't forget how she didn't want the Brighton day to end. Don't forget the star-shaped biscuits she baked exclusively for me, her 'star': I told myself. I had every reason to trust my feelings for Kathy were mirrored by hers for me.

Young feelings of love for a girl of twenty-three don't materialise out of nothing. Such powerful feelings don't exist in isolation.

Kathy was drawn to me, there was no denying it. The only question which remained was whether or not she could bring herself to accept reality.

She couldn't, apparently.

She didn't turn up. Rang half an hour after she was due, to say she wouldn't be coming.

I see her point: no sense in sharing feelings we couldn't do anything about. What good would that have done?

Kathy doesn't want to have to hold herself responsible for what happens to my marriage. Nor is she responsible, it's nothing to do with her. At most a catalyst, the innocent agent of necessary change, due neither credit nor blame.

You disagree: I know.

Do you ever pause to reflect what it must be like for Kathy living under permanent threat of attack from you? Maybe you should. Maybe you'd realise how unfair you're being. Have you noticed Kathy's thumbs, the quicks picked so badly sometimes she has to bandage them? She's not Superwoman, you know. She's a lovely, ordinary girl whose life you're making a misery without rhyme or reason. If you're looking for a scapegoat you've got one right here: me, your husband. If you've got to blame someone other than yourself blame me, not Kathy.

No! Please, I beg you not to blame yourself, my love. We've worked it out, haven't we? No one's to blame. It couldn't be any different from the way it is now, given the way it started. We *know* that. I can't bear your screams of pain. Won't they ever stop, won't the wounds ever heal?

My meeting with your mother was less upsetting than I'd feared. She seemed to know exactly what was happening. Did you ring her frequently from Glasgow? Or have I asked you that before? Too late now for an answer.

Lunch at the Design Centre was her idea, not mine. I guess she reckoned the choice of venue would please me. And so it might had she not insisted on looking antediluvian, dressed in the most outdated of her tailored tweed suits: the heatherish one with a tight skirt, flared below her knobbly knees.

Actually, I remember it feeling good to see the old bird. She does look a bit like a bird, being so thin and holding her head cocked to one side when she listens – not beautiful, like you. Your mother bought your father and me each a design-award trowel set – for my herb garden, she said. Things like that make me the saddest: the unused trowel set, shiny-bright in its red plastic box. I was OK till I recalled that; now I can hardly see for tears. Whinnying noises keep escaping through my nose.

Herb gardens? I don't cook any more. I haven't cooked a decent meal since we had the Hawthorns to dinner (plus the de Rougemonts, Frances and . . . can't remember whom she dragged along that evening). How many dinners do you reckon I cooked in Fifi's converted stables? One a fortnight on average for six years; that's a hundred and fifty. I haven't chopped a single sprig of dill since the Hawthorns came to dinner, soon after we returned from Agadir.

Your mother likes to see the world in pairs – not a perfect arrangement, she says, but the best on offer. At our minimalist lunch she came the closest I've heard her to admitting the problems with your father. She mentioned Kathy too, by name: which I thought was brave. Your mother has more faith in me than you have, you know. She understood how I wouldn't have been as foolish to imagine Kathy could supply all I had discovered lacking in our relationship. 'Nobody's perfect. Man or woman. Kathy has qualities Dinah lacks, no doubt. And vice versa, I'm sure. As I'm sure you're well aware': was how she put it. Your mother knows it's not Kathy that's the problem, it's us. She seemed to think there was more you needed to sort out in your mind than I did in mine. All through lunch she repeated her request for me to be patient with you, not to object if you took a flat on your own in town for a bit (which was what you said you wanted to do at the time). Your mother didn't seem anxious in herself – she was more concerned with how I was, with making certain I wasn't going to abandon our marriage just because of a temporary desire for separation. Every couple benefits from time apart, from time to time, she suggested. She said she wished she and your father had lived less on top of each other in the early years, his present weekday working absences in London being much the best arrangement.

Patience: I agree. I must above all else be patient.

Your mother is a great supporter of my work – always has been. She chatted about the Covent Garden campaign with a grasp of technical detail which surprised me; reminding me how closely I shared my career with you in those days, and how much you contributed to its success. It's true. I'd never have been anyone without you. Your unquestioning support in all I did made succeeding matter less. With you there to catch me if I faltered, with our us an unsinkable life-raft, I achieved things I would otherwise have dismissed as beyond my reach. Not being in the least bit worried if I did fail, I didn't. And you never let me stray from your encircling arms, my love, not once. Your love for me grew and grew, until I learnt to rely on our us as unassailable; until our us became the rock on which all that was important to me in life safely rested.

'You're sensible souls at heart': your mother said. What

did she mean? I thought I knew at the time – my mother would have said something like 'you shouldn't have taken so much for granted' – but I've no idea now. Heart? I'd rather not have had a heart. Probably haven't any longer – and better off for not. Sensible souls? Doesn't make sense, not to me. To you perhaps. I need reasons now not sentiment. You've told me you despise my father's wishy-washy optimism. What about your own? Time you faced the truth, you know.

I have.

I'm beginning to, I mean.

It's true to say – I think – that the Covent Garden success was yours, not mine. The excitement of anarchic plans laid in back-street pubs, of neighbourhood meetings, of door-to-door interviews on the iron staircases of tenement blocks, all those things we did together, even the articles themselves, were you not me. Although it was I who wrote the pieces for the paper, printed under my name in my column; I made my reputation with the Covent Garden reprieve, it's always said.

Did I? Or did you make my reputation for me?

What do *I* want to do?: that's what I'm trying to work out.

You think I know exactly what I want. You say I'm tramlined on selfish certainty. But it's not true, Dinah. I may know by now a good deal about what I don't want, very little though of what I do.

Your mother spoke at lunch of a couple's comfort in shared responsibility for the mundane decisions of day-to-day life, and of the sense of being cared for in marriage; a sort-of subliminal awareness of caring, she said, as it's not often – in your father's case – openly displayed. Michael Hawthorn also bangs on about responsibility. He says I'm morally responsible for looking after you because of the marriage vows – which I think is nonsense; and told him so. Michael took me out to lunch last week expressly to inform me he considers I'm making a terrible mistake, ruining my life. Nice of him to care. I hadn't realized how highly he rates you, thought he found you frivolous. ('Genetically incapable of taking women seriously,' you say he is – quoting Challis, no doubt.) He reckons I'll be lost without you.

If Michael hadn't been so critical I might have opened up

to him, might have talked to someone else for a change. All this self-chat: sometimes I'm afraid I'll go mad.

I hear from Frances you think I'm having a nervous breakdown.

If that's how you choose to explain it, go ahead – I'm beyond caring.

You needn't have been so cross with me about the house: I didn't particularly want to stay, just thought you'd prefer not to be there on your own, stifled by reminders of the life we could no longer lead. You accused me of plotting to deprive you of everything, the house as well as everything else – when it was you who first wanted to move out. You make it sound as though I'm the conductor of some netherworld orchestra, drawing lightning from the sky with a flick of my baton, a roll on the timpani burying you beneath a pile of garbage. I'm not God, you know. I can't be solely responsible, not for everything.

I'm sorry, I . . . Sorry? Why am I always apologising to you? Like a naughty boy. You're not my mother – you were meant to be my wife.

I don't mind where I live any more; although at the time it was – I admit – a wrench leaving home. You ordered me to take whatever I needed and clear out before you returned from Glasgow.

I didn't want much. Didn't wish, either, to destroy the place for your return. My own family things I took; and some of the stuff you never liked – the wicker chair from the spare bedroom, with a pink satin cushion (maybe it's the cushion Mum fancies, not the chair?). I carted my wok around in the boot of the car for weeks before dispatching that up to my mother too, plus the utensils and special Chinese sauces and things I used to buy in Soho.

I quite enjoyed packing up my books. For their memories: seldom in the actual stories on the page; more often in the circumstances of their reading, or being read to. Wilf's Arthur Ransome books removed from the highest of our glass shelves – in pastel coloured dust jackets, the tears repaired with Sellotape: *Coot Club, Secret Water, Swallowdale, We Didn't Mean To Go To Sea* – and others. Wilf (Brian

Wilford-Smith is his real name, the Rev Wilford-Smith since not so long ago) has always been my friend. Wilf raised us children to his own adult level – quite something, considering he's so tall and never married, so has none of his own. Playing devil's advocate against my mother's disciplined control, on my eighteenth birthday he sent a cheque for a hundred pounds with instructions I spend it in ways of which she would disapprove! Mum didn't object at all. 'Typical Wilf,' she laughed. It's possible Wilf was in love with my mother in the War and that her marriage to my father broke his heart. One hundred pounds was a lot of money in 1966, easily enough to take me down to the South of France and pay for my keep while I looked for a job on a yacht.

You've never liked Wilf, have you? 'How can a man with so much grease on his hair also have dandruff?' you once said, thinking you were being funny. I don't suppose he likes you very much either although he hasn't a word to say against you. Unlike friends of yours, with their stupid comments about me. Which of them is it, I'd like to know, who's saying you chucked me because I'm queer? Not sure whom I dislike most: whoever said it, or Pam Fisher – bitch – for telling me.

Before being ordained Wilf worked as bursar in various boys' schools – where we loved going to stay during the school holidays. Mum didn't worry about our playing in the walled safety of private grounds, and used to let us roam free all day. The roller-skating was fantastic – through deserted tarmac quadrangles and round and round the slippery concrete of covered fives courts, the steel of my clip-on skates screaming. Sarah-Jane's skates had rubber wheels, one of which was so stiff it barely turned. I made friends with the groundsmen and used to help them prepare the cricket pitches. Over morning tea in a big shed behind the pavilion – with mowers parked in graduated rows, and girlie cut-outs nailed to the wall – they smoked roll-your-own cigarettes and spat on the floor. A daughter of one of the groundsmen – I've just remembered – took down her knickers for me, behind the pile of cut grass at the back of the shed. Her bottom was snow-white, her woollen knickers black. Sarah-Jane told

Mum. Or maybe I told, I can't remember. She was furious and we were forbidden to play with the girl again.

I loved worm-casting, first thing in the morning before the sun dried the dew. The groundsmen cut me a half-size cane and I was allowed to work in line with them, pacing the field, swishing the cane across the grass to knock over the night's worm-casts. The canes made wonderful sounds whooshing in time across the wet grass and clattering into the tiny spirals of hardened earth. They only did it before important matches – when the school fields had been requisitioned for a county game, or a local club derby – so cricket balls wouldn't bobble awkwardly for the fielders. You could tell when one of us had missed a bit because the dew still shone in the sun. They never blamed me; which was kind of them as I had to struggle to keep pace, and they could surely see I skipped ground at times.

I took everything so seriously: listening so intently to their talk, not talking myself. I had my own mug – they called it mine. One wet afternoon, stuck in the shed with nothing much to do, the groundsmen made me a go-cart, using the wheels of an old pram. When Mum refused to let me take the go-cart home to York I cried and cried.

Why am I drawn tonight to write about childhood? Not what I'm meant to be doing at all.

Now it's haircuts – my head is busy with pictures of my first visit to the barber. Dad and I were fine till we returned home, quite enjoyed ourselves until we arrived back home and Mum was so terribly angry. With Dad, not with me. She shouted at him: terrible things. I've hated going to the barber ever since. Even now I'm guiltily fearful of bumping into my mother every time I have a hair cut . . .

I set out this evening to tell myself about leaving home – our home, not my parents'.

About packing into a tea-chest the stack of Ashmolean agendas, ten years of New Year gifts from your mother. She sent me one last year. Nothing this. Another of those heart-breaking images: a uniform run of desk diaries stretching from the year before our marriage began to the year before it looks like ending.

I'd hired a van and arranged to dump the tea-chests of

books, assorted suitcases of clothes and a few pieces of furniture – the bedside cabinet Mum gave me when I went up to Durham, my first grown-up possession – in New Cross with Lewis Bradstock, Gus's partner. I kept very little with me: typewriter; a worn-out briefcase full of bits and pieces from my desk, including the Great Exhibition paperweight ('one of the most ambitious, technically advanced and aesthetically far-sighted buildings England has ever seen', it says in a book the TLS has sent me to review – I quite agree); my Eames chair; the walnut travelling compendium; not much else. I didn't bother with any reference books.

All that fuss about bloody books: I can hear you chide.

It's ridiculous how little one actually needs.

Do you know what I did on my last night at home? I made myself a photograph album, pinched the unused album and stuck into it all the photographs I want to remember. Not just of you and me but from my childhood too, all the old photos I'd been storing in the compendium. It took several hours, and I wept continuously.

I'm glad I did it. When I look at the album now, whilst it can still make me cry, it also allows me to see our married years as an episode in life, not the whole of life itself. The album sets me free from you a bit, which is good. For you too my love, not bad. It's what I want, I suppose. To see if I can do it for myself.

My favourite photograph was taken by a total stranger who wandered onto the school fields at Wilf's one autumn morning. Sarah-Jane and I were playing French cricket with a boy called Richard, a master's son. We two had coats on; Richard wore a V-necked sweater, long socks crumpled to his ankles. I was cheating, holding the bat away from Sarah-Jane's legs – all three of us are laughing in the photograph. The man sent the prints to Wilf a few days later, in a plain brown envelope with neither name nor note. Soft-grained, home-developed prints. Wilf keeps his on his library mantelpiece, sharing a scuffed leather frame with his mother.

The last hour before leaving home I spent in your studio. Until a month or two ago I could recall at will the smell of your studio – now I require a prop, a prompt, the appearance on the stage of some particularly poignant memory to bring your you-ness fully to life. Then I can journey much further back: to the smell of your bedroom in Godstow where we escaped your mother's weekend guests to kiss. Your shy schoolgirl's smell, my Woolly, the scent of a grown-up schoolgirl.

Alastair was in a dreadful state when he arrived, late one December evening, to take up George and Susannah Forbes' offer of a room until early in the New Year, by which time he promised to make alternative arrangements. Greeting Alastair on the doorstep Susannah regretted not having kept a better eye on him, wished she had bent her rules never to interfere in other people's affairs unless asked (even then with a marked reluctance). Alastair, after all, was not 'other people': he was the only man in the world, apart from her father, the memory of whose loving she unconditionally cherished.

It both worried and annoyed her to find him in such a state, his handsome head of curly blondish hair unwashed, his face slumped. His neglect threatened social disintegration, the separation of body from mind. A heavy smoker herself Susannah forgave the stink of cigarettes on Alastair's jacket as he removed his coat in the hall – but not the sweaty tang of his overworn shirt, nor the whiff of stale urine rising from his crotch, an odour frighteningly familiar to Susannah from the gang of drunks who had taken over nearby Parsons Green, where she twice-daily walked their dog, a golden retriever the drunks insisted on petting. Alastair's appearance upset her. The neat, modestly fashionable pundit, the one public figure she could safely call a friend, had let things slip out of control, and Susannah doubted she could cope with daily evidence of his decline.

His sadness invaded the household; the whole neighbourhood: Susannah began to feel. Late one pre-Christmas night, following what the Forbes rated a successful dinner party – aromatic blends of Foreign Office and the media – Alastair stayed on in the drawing room playing records. At two in the morning he was still there, demolishing the cognac – or so George and Susannah wakefully suspected – and playing Pergolesi's *Stabat Mater* over and over again at maximum volume. At three George descended the stairs in his dressing gown to point out to Alastair that he was keeping half the street awake – and discovered him perched on the edge of a chair, wracked by a night-long sob the agonising sound of which he sought to drown in music.

From the way at any time of night or day, even in front of the children, Alastair was drawn to talk of Kathy, and from the vehemence with which he denied her causal role in his troubles, Susannah could see he had fallen chronically in love with the girl. She declined, however, to argue with him and concentrated instead on making sure his clothes were clean and that he ate well, drank less on the evenings he spent at home with them. Once the initial shock of sorrow for him subsided, Susannah felt perversely bolstered by her ex-boyfriend's distress: in relief that she herself was not personally involved, as she would have been – she was convinced – in this or something similar had she not abandoned him in Durham. She felt gratefully protected by her instincts, knowing now that Alastair would have been too much for her, that his undergraduate adoration could have ended only in pain. Or worse still: in collapse. There was nothing Susannah valued more highly than her capacity to remain in control of her own emotions; of George's and the children's too; of their doctored dog's also, most of the time.

In the depressive autumn of her last year at Durham, inwardly wearied by her contemporaries' competitiveness, by their intellectual point-scoring and cynicism, Susannah had warmed to the attention of the good-looking freshman in the library. To the smile in his eyes behind long lashes, alert to her daily arrival. To the frown of pretended disinterest when a friend approached for a whispered chat, or whisked her off for coffee – his face tellingly expressionless if the friend happened to be another man. One day she overheard his name. And another morning held his gaze and mouthed, 'Hello.' Alastair blushed. Susannah did not – to her lasting satisfaction. Dropping the pretence, they started to salute each other with surreptitious smiles, the second into the library always picking a place within sight of the first. At closing time – extended Tuesday-through-Thursday to nine o'clock – on a wintry night shortly before the end of term Susannah sensed his steeling himself to say something. She quickened the desultory packing of notes and books into her music case (calculated compromise between plastic bag and Gladstone) and set off for the door slightly ahead of him. When she half-turned in the hall outside, he invited her for a drink in the old wine house in Market Square, where she discovered he was less sporty in conversation than in looks. Suzanne: Alastair had mistakenly thought she was called, and claimed – charmingly – much to prefer Susannah. She felt idiotically happy that he liked her name.

The purity of his passion for her, his categorical belief in the efficacy of love proved irresistible and by Easter Susannah found herself responding with the same delicate touches of the fingertips, the same barrage of letters, the same extravagant declarations of devotion. As if the passion was her own instead of – as she subsequently realised – principally his, loaned to her so she could reflect it back at the correct choreographed moment. He managed to make their closeness seem natural and inevitable; when in reality it was wholly contrived. With the previous man in her life Susannah had felt the entire fabric of his male pride and authority depended on her simulated inability to resist his driving sexual urge. Alastair, in contrast, attempted to seduce her without once reaching with his hand between her legs. Alastair and she made love fully clothed, on the rug in front of her gas fire; he ejaculating in his jeans, she – spreadeagled beneath him, miniskirt hitched to her waist – coming in her panties. They did share one whole night together, the night of the Union Ball, the early morning hours of which they spent in bed in his Mark Street digs – where he lent her a pair of his pyjamas, and kissed her nipples through a gap in the buttons.

If only Alastair had taken account of how she intrinsically felt their almost-love might have survived two years apart, while he completed his degree and she took a job in London. He was, in his way, very sensitive – more so than her husband. Much of what Alastair did for himself had been pleasing for her: his pace, particularly, and his softness. If only he had stopped from time to time to check how she was feeling everything could have been all right. It was attention Susannah lacked, not satisfaction.

There was no doubt in Susannah's mind that Alastair had cared for her. Look at the bunch of fresh market flowers he contrived to leave on the front mat of her London flat the morning of her birthday – with George already established in her bed: she assumed he must have suspected. Look at the letters he wrote, telling her how wrong she was to defy a love like theirs. Wrong in principle: he sought to persuade.

Love, though, was not enough, not nearly enough for Susannah.

Susannah had no illusions, recognised life as seldom less than a continuous struggle. Within her blinkered field of vision the world was a tense ungiving place where a woman's most significant duty, her *raison d'être* was to defend advantage for her own: for her children, basically, and for George, their provider. Susannah grasped all the privileges class and money could provide, the horror-lesson of what poverty meant, of what she was convinced would happen to her if she were for a moment to let go, belched in her face by the drunks on Parsons Green. Life was easier abroad, where the Foreign Office paid for help in the house and provided wives with cars – chauffeur driven in Pakistan – and where George operated with the assurance of a man destined for the top. Back home, on secondment to the Ministry of Defence, George's status seemed less elevated; and Susannah felt positively deprived compared with contemporaries whose husbands did something in the City (toothless wives of the dullest men drove BMWs – rather fast, she noticed). The shame of not being able to afford the best in their thirties would be recompensed by George's 'K' in their fifties: she comforted herself. Sir George and Lady Susannah Forbes had just the right resonance – worth any number of second cars. It had lately crossed her mind, however, that George might lack the ultimate push, the fine cutting edge of careermanship to make it to Ambassador. Susannah wondered if she should make him jump ship now and take some sinecure in the City, before he was too old to succeed there either.

George's flaws could have made Susannah very angry had she allowed them to, the same amiable mediocrity reproducing itself in tubby miniature in her son. Janet, their eldest child, was altogether sturdier, more like her grandmother. Watching her teenage daughter reach out towards the newly liberated world, where women were permitted an existence of their own, Susannah quite often felt jealous. Given a chance to live life over again she might well have decided to be a success herself: a presenter of breakfast time TV, maybe, or a glittering literary agent. There were lots of possibilities these days.

In her day, despite a respectable degree and the missionary example of her eccentric mother, Susannah had merely flirted with an independent career, her ambitions centred on one job alone: that of wife-and-mother. A picture of polite indifference to other aspects of male chauvinism, Susannah bridled at the dinner table solely when some bellied businessman remarked: 'Ah, you don't work, then' in response to her telling him about the children. Any other insult she stoically ignored, or deflected with a flattering aside – the diplomat's perfect consort – but the stupidity, the sheer injustice of anti-motherhood remarks infuriated her. Most men were aware how exhausting the management of house and family was in practice. Knowing that men knew this helped make the job worth the trouble, made mildly endearing a husband's stunning incompetence on the few occasions he might be obliged to run the home. But it was wrong, much more serious than simply offensive, for a man publicly to belittle the mother's role.

Marriage, on Susannah's terms, was not a compromise but a pact, an arrangement of equal and necessary benefit to both parties. George appreciated the nature of their relationship, readily accepting his wife's authority on matters of family significance. George, Susannah acknowledged, was precisely the husband she had planned on having: wholly unobjectionable, even when it came to sex. Susannah had succeeded in circumscribing their love-making from the first genital contact, preserving to herself wide swathes of privacy around the monthly cycle and her two carefully calculated pregnancies. All the same, she prided herself on being 'good in bed', on making it all – on nights when it was allowed – as easy for George as he could wish, judging her mock groans and astute vaginal pressure to optimum effect. Every six weeks or so she prolonged the performance, and when she finally brought him to orgasm scratched her fingernails down his back, aware of the gain in self-esteem due love-marks sported in the shower room at the RAC after his swim. It was part of the pact: her task to do the loving. In married life she did not expect others' – husband's or childrens' – love to be demonstrably returned, did not want them openly to love her back. Disdaining the public touch of intimacy, Susannah kept passion on a leash.

She felt safe with George. The only men to have seduced her into open demonstrations of affection – first her father, then Alastair – had threatened her sense of self-control. All the same, Alastair's extended stay with them in Parsons Green set

Susannah to comparing him and George. Was she right to have chosen safety?

Her mother had always favoured Alastair. 'Now this one really does have a future', she had said of Alastair – whilst later describing George, in a xeroxed Christmas circular to friends abroad, as 'dutifully devoted'. A measure of her mother's attraction to Alastair could be taken from the fact that the only time Susannah heard her mention the Visitation to anyone outside the Lowland Band of Brethren was in conversation with Alastair. On the Easter visit home from Durham her mother told him how a messenger called from the Lord and ordered her to visit an unfamiliar house in a nearby village, where she discovered an old lady within hours of death by starvation, immobilised at the foot of her stairs by a hip broken in a fall. 'There's no mistaking a visit from the Lord,' Susannah overheard her mother say to Alastair. 'And it's the eternal Hell Fires unless he calls.' No one escapes on Judgement Day, Mrs Appleton explained. Although she herself had been summoned to His side, her three daughters, her son, her runaway husband, Alastair too, were all currently condemned to burn in Hell. Wasn't that a bit unfair? Alastair protested. What if he was knocked down and killed in the street tomorrow before God found time to visit him? Susannah's mother laughed. 'Nice young man like you, maybe He'll come to you as you go.'

Susannah was convinced she could have coped with Alastair better than Dinah had managed. Unlike the couple's adoring circle of close friends, she had always detected in Alastair a certain shiftiness, a distinct unwillingness to pronounce himself content. Although she had met Dinah once only – at a party hosted by the Shores the previous autumn in a Bloomsbury gallery – Susannah was left with the impression that Dinah was a difficult woman, a woman not to be crossed. Confrontation was inevitable with a woman of Dinah's temperament, Susannah tried to explain to Alastair. He should take steps to protect himself.

Alastair was himself partly responsible for the situation, Susannah acknowledged. By spending so many evenings at Roxeth House, within spitting distance of his vacated home and deserted wife, Alastair courted disaster. It was all very well to establish the Home as out of bounds for Dinah – a condition to which he claimed she had meekly aquiesced – but did this not smack of a direct challenge to transgression? Here is my chin, hit it: he might almost have been saying.

The challenge, if challenge it was, Dinah took up – in the Brasserie in Greenwich where Alastair and she met one evening to discuss financial matters. Susannah heard about the incident later that same night, when Alastair returned to Parsons Green in an unhideable state of distress. She sat him down on a kitchen stool, with a tumbler of Scotch, and made him tell her what had happened. For no apparent reason Dinah – Alastair maintained – lost control in the middle of the meal and shouted obscenities at him at the top of her voice, employing a violence of language he never dreamt she possessed. She threatened to kill him – and Alastair believed her capable of it. Dinah finished up in blind hysteria, and had to be dragged away to the Ladies by two of the waitresses.

The shocked and yet, in the same breath, exultant manner in which Alastair related the story made Susannah suspect he wished to provoke reactions from which there could be no turning back. In permitting herself the indignity of public collapse Dinah deserved to suffer the consequences: was Susannah's harsh conclusion.

Greeted by defensive antagonism to offers of advice, Susannah confined comment on Alastair's endlessly repetitive monologues to what she considered the most relevant subject at that stage: money. If it came to a divorce Dinah would screw Alastair for every penny he possessed, Susannah warned. Dinah had no right to strip Alastair of the financial security hard work had earned him; not with her wealthy family behind her; and without children, when eminently capable of earning a living for herself. Susannah tried to make Alastair see sense, make him understand that he owed his wife nothing.

'You're wrong,' he said. 'Money has never mattered to us. It's not the money she wants. It's me.'

Thinking back to their time together, to those two and a half indulgently romantic terms in Durham before life for her began in earnest, Susannah realised how little Alastair had changed. He had always been careless with money, generous both to himself and to friends when he had it and oblivious to its absence when he hadn't. Susannah smiled in recall of the expensive pair of cavalry twills he bought for the visit to her mother in Troon. Such a kid: transparently proud of the figure he cut in his new trousers, so pleased to feel the part – unaware his shoes gave him away. To say nothing of his horizontally striped tie! Susannah frowned at another memory: his gift to her of the etched glass decanter (already full of *La Ina*) on the night of the Union Ball. She valued the decanter not merely as a memento of nearly being in love; she adored its integral beauty.

Alastair's beautiful decanter, standing on a silver tray in the drawing room, comforted Susannah in panic moments of aloneness – by reminding her of a time when she knew for certain she was loved. No one else had loved her with such accuracy as to present her with a gift she could forever safely cherish.

I can understand – now – why you were so upset about my leaving behind the love-dolls. At the time I rationalised the insult by telling myself they represented a crucial phase in your work which you'd want to keep to show clients. Needing more than one excuse, I persuaded myself they were yours not mine – even though you wove them for me, in secret, when I won the Granville Award.

You're right: I've never liked them. I think they're vulgar. Call me a prude, but they *are* vulgar, gratuitously explicit.

You're one of those people who always has to be right – like my mother, in that respect. Mum never makes mistakes, does everything immaculately. I could never get anything completely right for her; however well I did, something would always be wrong. When I won my All England Schools Trophy, guess what her first words to me were? 'Do wipe your nose, darling.'

Your telephone calls at work almost destroyed me. Especially in the morning, the day's intake of nicotine as yet to marshal its effect, my head swimming in the previous night's drink. At eight every morning these days I go for a swim in our local pool (where the cashier fancies me). You didn't do it on purpose, I know; you were in agony yourself. It was the loving things you said, anyway, which crucified me, not the abuse. Don't let yourself be overwhelmed by my love for you, my Woolly: you used to beg. You knew what it was I was running away from, you see. I didn't. I'd escape from the office and pace up and down St Michael's Churchyard, tears pouring down my cheeks. A Deacon, I think he must have been, linked an arm through mine once and walked with me, in silence, till I'd calmed down. I imagined I was thinking in crystal clarity – but I wasn't; I was in a terrible mess. While you spoke on the phone of evil forces dividing our kindred spirits I'd gaze about my featurewriter's cubicle, with your V & A poster Sellotaped to the door, thinking: she's right, she's absolutely right, what I'm doing is madness, is death. But I didn't tell you I agreed. And I didn't let anyone see, through the office's glass walls, my tortured confusion. Sometimes you blamed yourself. I remember your saying you'd heard the sounds you made: like a gramophone record with the needle stuck in the same groove of complaint: about your work, and the impossibility of producing anything worth the effort. A piercing, moaning screech: you called it. Agonising for those – like me, you said – who cared but could not help.

The paper flower-chain which I took from your dressing table mirror hangs by the poster on the door. The pink flowers and green leaves have faded to a uniform dusty cream.

I didn't stop you ringing. I encouraged you. Told you how much I wanted to share your pain, how much I wished to help. I felt certain I was acting for us both. It seemed impossible I could be doing all that, inflicting such ruin unless you, deep down, wanted me to go – despite your clamour for my return. Where could I have found the strength to do it on my own? You were pushing me, you must have been.

I've got a letter of yours here in my hand, criticising me for my coldness on the telephone. *Your distant tones disconnect us word by word*: you wrote.

Your Christmas letter nearly brought me home – not the heartbreaking content alone, but the fact of it being Christmas, family time in Godstow. The letter opened straight in at the top of the paper – no 'My love', no 'Darling Woolly'. *I don't know what to call you any more*: you began. The familiar terms no longer meant anything, you said. You couldn't address me as 'my' anything because I wasn't yours, I'd turned my back on you. You still felt mine if I wanted you to be – but I didn't want you. You'd given yourself to me kiss by kiss until I'd drunk you dry and thrown you out. An empty skin. A vacant space. A seedless pod. Untouchable, unfeelable, unlovable. You would never love again: you maintained. Your flow of love had run dry.

Dear You you've ended up addressing my letters.

And 'you' it is I've been writing to these weeks.

I think I'll stop. I'm sure I'd best stop addressing you and start talking directly to myself.

You aren't you to me any, longer, not if I'm honest. You're Dinah.

You . . . Dinah I mean, *Dinah* saw it before I did; admitted it before I did, talked about it before I did. I was so taken up with satisfying myself Kathy wasn't to blame that I pretended the power of 'us' steamed on undiminished, long after I'd dismisssed to myself the practical reality, thrown our us back in Dinah's face.

The Christmas tree incident brought me to my senses, forced me to concede the loss of the rock, the life-raft, the all and only. Made me aware of the need to concentrate exclusively on you – Dinah – and push Kathy into the wings. I saw, for the first time, a danger that Dinah might not make it in one piece to the other side. I had to be totally available, to help her across.

Dinah's destruction of the Roxeth House Christmas tree must have been frightening to witness for those – everyone except me, I suspect, and her mother maybe – who knew only the fun-loving Dinah, the let's-make-the-party-swing Dinah.

I can see her point. She drops in to Roxeth House one morning – having first telephoned to make sure I didn't happen to be around – with a basket of beautifully wrapped presents for her friends, and finds life happily progressing to pattern, as if she might never have existed.

'Come and see the tree, dear,' Matron apparently said. 'Biggest ever.'

Dinah gives her heart to celebration, gathering in isolated spirits to share her warmth. Seeing the Roxeth House Christmas tree dressed in the decorations she'd collected over the years must have torn her in two. A dagger thrust into her bowels, slicing up through her lungs to the throat.

The giant paper crackers she and I had made together two years previously bore the brunt of her outrage. She tore them from the branches and ripped them apart, stamping and screaming and weeping. Then she must suddenly have seen the ridiculous side of things – a ring of pale staff, feet screwed to the floor in fear – for she started to laugh, patted Matron on the shoulder, apologised, handed over her parcels and walked back home to the studio.

It's anger. But at what? I know I let her down disgustingly, built up her belief in us then rejected it. Without warning.

Enough to justify her wanting to kill me?

Maybe it is.

What can I do?

I know: nothing. Although I didn't know that then. Then I thought I could leave her and love her, hurt her and heal her, love Dinah and love someone else.

No wonder I made her angry.

I'm not sure I can manage it: this 'her', this 'Dinah'.

Who am I writing for if it isn't you?

For myself.

For *myself*: must remember that.

I was least unhappy those days – evenings, I should say – at Roxeth House. In their wayward hopefulness the women there seemed to keep such a firm hold on the realities of life.

I could have listened to Mabel for hours, leaning against the window frame, half an eye out for Kathy's slim figure in the drive – her dreamed-of return: to prove nothing had really happened.

'Take a pew,' Mabel used to say.

'No, I'm just going. Carry on. Don't let me interrupt the story.'

Since becoming bedridden Mabel's principal source of enjoyment has rested with telling the other residents stories of the 'goings-on' in Roxeth House in the days when she used to char for Mr Bridge and 'that no-good Albert Mace'. 'In this very room!' she would declare, waving a rolled-up newspaper at the ceiling.

One evening I heard her describe, in technicolour detail, arriving at work to find an opera-hatted Albert (Amazing Mace, his stage name) asleep on the mat inside the door.

'Stank to high heaven. Shat himself hadn't he?' she shouted at the circle of old women who had been wheeled in for their evening's entertainment.

'You're telling fibs again,' Miss Gaydon rapped.

'God's truth. Show you the stain on the mat. Took me all morning to clean him up. Still drunk he was. Old sod.'

At that point Mabel stopped, puzzlement clouding her cataract-filmed eyes. 'Might've been my Dad,' she said. 'Can't quite remember right. He was a drinker too. All them men are, aren't they?'

Then she laughed. Everything ends in a laugh with Mabel.

'Only thing they're any bloody good at!'

I wonder if Mabel has any children? If she has she never mentions them. As no one visits her, who can I ask? She'd have made an ideal mother: with her cackling acceptance of ugliness in life, of weakness. Strength weakness, weakness strength. The strong protect the weak, mothers their sons – so successfully in my case that I'm too weak to look after anyone else, not Dinah even, nor the child she craved. I give the impression of being decisive, confident, independent-minded and all the other things I was brought up to believe are important. But I'm not. I'm not any of them.

Kathy wouldn't require me to be anyone other than who I am, the weakness alongside the strength. You can be yourself too with me Kathy, my lovely Kathy: I promise. Those fears, on my birthday picnic, of being a mere reflection, a mirror to others, that's not true. Two serious, quiet, solitary people we'd be, sharing our lives, our creativity and our concerns truthfully. No performances. No pretences.

Give it time, she said.

How long? How long does she expect me to be able to wait?

I'm not afraid. If it's not going to be her it'll be no one. There's plenty of good I can do on my own. I don't wait emptily for Kathy to make her way back to Roxeth House; I'm getting on with things: she'll see. The Appeal's progressing – over half-way there. I've managed very well for myself. Given up smoking; swim thirty lengths non-stop crawl every morning, Sundays too; resigned from that Crafts Council committee . . . lots of things. She'll see, she'll see.

I'll soon be my own self. Then Kathy will agree to be with me.

Wilf advised me, when I went to stay with him that Christmas, to try and think more about myself. He warned me that I needed to be clear for myself before I could hope to solve anyone else's problems.

I still need reminding today: to talk to myself instead of to Dinah; to talk *about* Dinah perhaps, but not *to* her.

I never loved Dinah for herself, I loved her for loving me.

I love Wilf for himself, I reckon.

I love his grey-green tweed jackets, which already look faded when they're brand new. I love his jars of expensive jam: at tea in the library, a bog-oak crucifix fixed to the wall near the door, his Prayer Book resting on a narrow *prie-dieu*, and the glazed bookcase – too massive for the modern bungalow the Parish Council persuaded him to move into – at the far side, stuffed with interest. With cookery books, for instance. Wilf has three or four marvellous early books on cooking, a subject he's quite knowledgeable about. Yet he eats almost entirely from tins and packets; powdered 'Smash' potatoes – the row of King Edwards in the vicarage garden he prefers to give away to village pensioners too sick to grow things for themselves. He never lets me lift a finger in the kitchen; nor shows the slightest embarrassment at serving up such muck.

When I was in confirmation class at school Wilf used to send me unusual prayers to transcribe into a special notebook. I can't recall a single prayer now – not that I've ever been any good at remembering such things: verses to recite; jokes to tell; songs to sing.

I remember the motto Gran wrote in Sarah-Jane's autograph book.

Good Better Best
Never Let it Rest
Until Your Good Is Better
And Your Better Best.

I can picture the inscription as clear as anything, in Gran's rounded hand on a blue page in the multi-coloured book. *Good Better Best* . . . That's what I've done all my life; not for myself but for other people, in order to please other people. Bribing them to love me.

It's time I grew up.

I used to believe that Dinah's way of dealing with life was self-evidently better than mine – not better in a moral sense, better in practice: for her; for me; for everyone around. It never crossed my mind that the real Dinah might be no better than the real me. Might be worse, in some ways. Bad for me, anyway.

When I left Susannah's – a year ago last January – and moved in with the Cartwrights in Highbury Grange, Dinah abandoned any effort to control her telephone calls. At midnight she'd ring, then again at two in the morning: to tell me I'm weak, worthless, worse than a murderer. I'd be standing in my pyjamas in the cold trying to calm her down, desperate for the means to make her understand I still loved her. Pierced through by her pain, I'd scrabble in the dark for a key back into her heart. The nearest telephone to my bedroom – in the attic of Belinda's Victorian terrace house – was two flights down, on the girls' landing. Annie, the eldest daughter, who before Christmas had started her first full-time job in an Islington pasta bar, said she couldn't believe how patient I was with Dinah on the phone. Eavesdropping from her bed behind the door, Annie cried too – in empathy. None of her boyfriends had said anything half as loving to her, she told me. She wasn't in the least bit surprised Dinah refused to let me go.

They lasted half an hour, longer sometimes, those dreadful telephone calls – mostly putting right third-party misrepresentations. What did our friends think they were doing? Why couldn't they have said they didn't know, instead of trying to explain to her my behaviour?

It must have been awkward for them, I realise. She was like an addict: addicted to me, to my thoughts, my words, how I looked, who I was seeing, what I was saying, how I was feeling . . . And they told her whatever sounded comforting, whatever it seemed Dinah most wanted to hear.

It's standard stuff. Nothing unique about us, about our sadness; it happens to everyone.

Although – to be honest – I still can't help feeling there was a certain magic centred in our us. All our friends remarked on it: the most joyful wedding they'd ever attended, the source of much-repeated reminiscences. In the church, waiting for Dinah and her father to arrive, there was such a hubbub the vicar had to intervene. 'Excuse me!' he shouted. 'You're in church not at a cocktail party. An attitude of prayer is meant to greet the bride. Of prayer!'

The first phone call I made from Highbury Grange was to Mr Abraham: to leave my new address and telephone number in case Kathy needed to be in touch. I wrote to her that night too, the final letter commendably short after first composing a *cri de coeur* – not sent, thank God, or there'd be no chance of her wanting to see me.

Want? I can't believe she doesn't want to see me. It's whether she'll risk giving rein to her emotions. Maybe she's afraid my love will be too much for her? Maybe I've got to learn to love her less not more? To love her better – then best.

I admire Belinda Cartwright – for her unflappability. She's not perfect. Her faults – as known to me, there may be others – are: dirty neck, bitten fingernails, lack of discipline with the children, failed marriage, provocative underwear, cheats on the Underground, chews gum, doesn't get up in time for a proper breakfast before work, keeps fat so long in the frier it stinks, reads the *New Statesman*, plays tennis too well for a woman, athletes foot, hopeless friends, always asking me whether I'm hungry. Her failings also define her qualities. Being genuinely interested in people she's tremendously patient with us all. With Mick too, her ex-husband. A Do-It-Yourself fanatic – the sort that starts the next task before finishing the one before last – Mick left the house in Highbury Grange littered with his improvements. There are no rules at Belinda's: friends come and go as they please. She's the neighbourhood's Agony Aunt. When Mick stays to supper – once a week at least – he too pours his heart out to her over the dishes, much as he used to while they were married I imagine. He discusses all his love affairs with her the latest: a bus driver with a sexy silver tooth). Mick is still repaying in instalments the four hundred pounds Belinda invested in his bankrupt Pie 'n' Mash shop on the Balls Pond Road.

Belinda and her three girls talk openly to me about sex. I knew women nattered a lot about sex – just amongst themselves though, I thought; not to men too. All four Cartwrights are totally uninhibited. Caroline is only sixteen and Belinda lets her boyfriend spend the night in her room – weekends only: not to interfere with O' level revision.

There's a packet of Tampax on display in the downstairs loo, beside the spare toilet rolls.

I can't remember when I first learnt about women having periods. Too late to avoid mistakes.

We were on the beach at Bridlington, on joint holiday with Auntie Sylvia, Cheryll and Roland. Cheryll and I were thirteen. We adored each other, and on a such a hot day I couldn't understand her refusal to come swimming with me. I kept on at her all day long, pleading for an explanation. Did she have a cold? Was Auntie Sylvia punishing her for something she'd done wrong? Weren't we friends any more? 'Tell him! Why won't you tell him?' she hissed at the grown-ups, and ran off to read a book in the car. 'Leave her alone, Al. There's a good boy,' my father said. Mum jumped to her feet: 'Come on, let's look for shells.'

Wandering across the sand with my mother I forgot about Cheryll – whom I haven't much liked since.

I already knew, as a child, about the existence of sanitary towels, stained yellowy-red with muck and blood. I knew there were cords attached at either end – although I couldn't work out what the cords were meant to be tied to. Suspender belt? A memory, a genuine childhood memory: not handed down to me in some jolly story, recorded for our album by the box Brownie. I remember the pitch of my mother's exclamation on finding the mess had seeped through – once – to her cotton skirt. Though I'd no idea what the blood between my mother's legs signified it didn't in itself frighten me. At least I don't think it did. It was her apparent anger at it all which made me afraid. My mother's periods caused me more distress than anything else in my enclosed childhood world. Or am I imagining things? Has Dinah's anguish stretched my nerves so taut I'm losing my grip?

My earliest memory – very early, as a baby – is of Mum's breast. I know it's a true image, not invented, because of the breast's scale resting white and full above my nose, a nest of blue veins wriggling away from the exposed surface into her flesh. The nipple bigger than my eye; stitched, it appeared, to her skin. I remember the different touches too: the rough brush of the nipple's side, and its hot centre where my tongue teased her milk; the caress of her breast against my head, pillowed for satiated sleep. Best of all I remember her sweat smell of maternal warmth. The smell of my mother I reckon to be the most beautiful thing on earth.

Belinda's attic room belonged to her nephew – Kent – who was away on a Police Cadet Course. His posters remained pinned to the walls, his books on the shelves; an Airfix model of the Mississippi paddle steamer *Robert E Lee* stood on top of his chest of drawers. In this borrowed boy's room I retreated, in my agony, back beyond adolescence to babyhood. I used to lie in a foetal ball on the floor, rocking on the points of my hip and shoulder bones. Not groaning, nor sobbing, but drawing breath in a whinny into my lungs. Or did I let air out? It's difficult to recall precisely. Amazing that I could forget the precision of that pain – the unquenchable ache of doubt, disbelief and despair. Dinah finds it almost as difficult to accept her survival from the horrors of sadness as she did the pain itself. How is it possible, she wrote the other day, that something she knew in her heart was death could turn out not to be? She was certain, once, that she'd love me forever; then equally certain that she'd never cease, for a second, hating me; and now she feels nothing – can barely recall what either hate or love is.

We were terrified of change: that was our trouble. We built our us to last unaltered to eternity.

I'm less frightened now.

Answering Belinda's scrawled advertisement on the NFT noticeboard was, in its small way, a plea for change, a testing of alternatives. Even after meeting her – one of those women with bulldozer hips, shrivelled breasts and vast spectacles who've always overawed me – and seeing the state of the room, I still dared try it out. Lots of things have changed. My use of the National Film Theatre is progress: watching films for their own sake, without needing always to make gainful use of my time. And I've acquired a new carelessness about my public image: it doesn't worry me at all that I might appear as odd to observant eyes as the other regulars at the NFT do to me – limping Jack Wilkinson and his band of buffs; and the bag-lady, shy of human touch. Frankly, these days I give little thought to the public impact of my articles. Bash them out on autopilot. And no one notices. Won a Press Council Award again this year just the same.

Learning, in these pages, to accept the existence of life inside my own head is the most serious thing I do.

Two years ago if anyone had told me Lewis Bradstock and I had much in common I'd have felt insulted – there seemed no purpose to his existence. These days I often drop in to see him on my way to Roxeth House. Just for a chat, without needing an excuse: the rescue of a book from my tea-chests. He's always there, in his steamy office, awaiting trade. Couriers are the newest fashion in the antiques business: Lewis says. Couriers make special appointments after hours – to impress their tame Yanks, sticking numbered labels on container-loads of junk. Lewis slips his best couriers a cash backhander to top up the official commission.

Lewis' type used to make me feel uneasy, the anarchy of their laziness, of their amused indifference to convention frightening me. I used to be frightened of them all, all the hippies and pop groupies and flower people and Hari Krishnas, afraid of their superior experience. At one time I suspected Lewis of being a cog in the drug machine. Actually, I'm still suspicious of him in this context (it's the mammoth joints he rolls) but the idea of it no longer frightens me: that's the difference.

Lewis plays the Indian flute at concerts in upper rooms of the ICA.

I enjoy talking to him. Utterly unconcerned about the people I mention – about me, even – his comments have the ring of truth.

Susannah can't believe how much I've changed. It's either that, she says, or else she never really knew me in the first place.

My attitude to Kathy has changed too; although my feelings for her haven't altered one bit, grown deeper if anything. I admire – inexpressibly – the dignity with which she has handled all this.
    I can't stop myself dreaming of her. Don't wish to. The same dreams month after month.
    I measured missing her in days then. Tomorrow we'll be together, tomorrow I'll fold her in my arms: I imagined.
    We meet now only in dreams.
    We walk in fields in my dreams, the warm breeze blowing a silky skirt against her thighs. Our bare arms brush, mine tanned hers pale. Hand in hand we walk up into the sheltered corner of a lush green field of grass: to make love in the sun. We make love at the centre of a wood, the ground softened by years of fallen leaves. We make love in hay ricks. And on a sailboat deck at sunset.
    I love you, Kathy. I love you. I love you. And you love me. I know you love me too.

The only time my father ever mentioned sex was to warn me of the naughty things the 'big boys' at Hillhead would try to do with my private parts. I was to resist at all costs, he said. Boys playing with each other's penises was evil. Bad enough, according to my father, to play with your own penis, an activity he personally has never – not once in his whole life – indulged in: he claimed.
    I believe him. I've never thought about it seriously before, but now that I have I believe him.

Drink drove me to call at the Abraham's flat in Hammersmith. Kathy's neglect, her not commenting on the proof of our Roxeth House pamphlet incensed me. For weeks I'd been disciplining myself not to worry. Telling myself that as soon as she saw how well our work had turned out, once she held the physical evidence in her hands, then she'd contact me and fulfil the promise to share her thoughts. A first night I gave her, plus two days grace for the post to catch up with wherever she was living.

I'd taken to the whisky bottle on my own in the office in the evenings. A pretence at extra work – really to occupy the hours before deciding where to eat. My favourite used to be the Simah Kebab House in Euston Road, where the owner's child, in her smart school uniform, scribbled at a corner table. I used to watch her for ages after I'd finished eating; anything to delay my return to play lodger in Belinda's Boys Own attic. Maybe it was a fit of anger, catching me unprepared which led me to the door of Mr Abraham's mansion flat by Hammersmith flyover.

He was very civil – considering; a mild, academic-looking man in a cardigan. I stood in the dim communal hall of Kathy's childhood home and harangued her father, ticked him off for his daughter's failure to face up to her responsibilities. He agreed. Said she'd always been difficult to control. As soon as I reached the bottom of the stairs, after wishing him a sullen good night, I immediately rushed back up and rang the bell again: to beg him not to tell Kathy I'd called. Mr Abraham agreed it would be better not to mention it. He was very nice.

I was sick in the gutter beside my car – the first (and last) time for years. Dinah sticks a finger down her throat and up it instantly comes. I can't. The sick reaches my tonsils and then subsides, leaving behind a sweet sting at the base of my tongue.

I dream of being father to Kathy's child. I do. It's crazy I know, but I do. I dream of holding our baby in my arms, and making myself into a perfect father.

Dinah has seen Kathy.

Dinah told me herself, rang up and asked me to call round for a Saturday tea in the studio. She sounded calm, and promised to remain so – so I agreed. Anyhow I was desperate, at the time, for information about Kathy.

The studio was as I'd left it five months earlier. Dinah kept her word about remaining calm. Acted soft and concerned, assuring me it was for my own good she was telling me all this, not to entice me back. She knew, she reiterated, that Kathy wasn't our problem, was a symptom not the cause. It was to save me pinning my hopes to a groundless dream that she had invited me for tea: she said.

Kathy pities me: Dinah told me – in a hushed voice, as if to a child.

'Kathy feels nothing for you but pity. I'm sorry, Woolly. But that's what she said.'

It's not true.

Although I don't think Dinah made it up. She looked too pleased with herself for it to have been a lie. Kathy must have said it – or something similar – to placate her, to help rid Dinah of the obsession. Kathy must have realised that until Dinah stops thinking all the time of the mythical 'other woman' she'll never get round to sorting herself out.

Kathy is so clear, so sure – it's wonderful. I feel incredibly lucky: first Susannah, then Dinah, now Kathy. More loving than any man deserves.

I'll earn it by doing something sensational. Not sure what. A TV series which opens the eyes of the world to the environment, private as well as public? The macrocosm of city a reflection of the microcosm of home. Since technology became the answer people have ceased to think about the question.

Something extraordinary to justify the pain. I'm going to do something extraordinarily important – with Kathy's help, I will.

According to Dinah, Kathy says it's not her at all that I've fallen in love with but some ideal in my head. Dinah says Kathy says I never saw the real her at all. It's happened before, Kathy says, men losing their hearts to the person they imagine her to be.

According to Dinah, Kathy doesn't intend ever to see me again. Doesn't intend to offer me a single word of explanation. Dinah says Kathy plans to disappear from my life completely: so that sooner or later I'll have no choice but to forget about her. The sooner the better Dinah says Kathy says.

No. Kathy knew I'd know it isn't true.

I'm waiting. Until the time comes when Kathy feels able to tell me the truth. She needs to be sure my love for her is genuine, not an excuse for leaving my marriage. She's thinking of me not of herself. Lovely, unselfish Kathy.

If she didn't love me she'd have told me so. 'Listen to what I say myself, not to what other people say I say,' she lectured me at Roxeth House when I over-reacted to a snide remark of Matron's.

Kathy's silence is a clear message of love, as clear as the kiss she solicited at the office door.

Geraldine Pollard worried about her daughter. She was concerned about Alastair too, towards whom she had felt fondly from the moment he first walked, shyly confident, into the drawing room at Godstow. Geraldine tried to conceal her concern – not for reasons of propriety, but because she wished the two of them to concentrate on themselves and not bother a jot how or what anybody else might think. It disturbed her to feel that Alastair's single-mindedness, his ferocious powers of self-delusion might prevent him abandoning this mistaken path; a path which led – Dinah's mother did not doubt – to the darkened half-world of aloneness. There was nothing much she felt able to do, no advice she could locate worth giving (not that it would have been heard, for both of them were bad at accepting advice, the mildest expression of alternative opinion taken as personal criticism). Geraldine decided she could best help by listening to them on the telephone, through their letters, and in the promptings of her maternal instinct – by listening to them and holding safe their confidences.

Not all mothers knew their daughters as well as she knew hers. Some mothers – most, perhaps, Geraldine suspected – were surrogately dedicated to the satisfaction of their own desires, not their daughters'. Where Dinah appeared to outsiders securely extrovert, her mother knew this hid – not a lack of self-esteem exactly – knew that this hid, what? That the inner motivation for her daughter's brightness, her sociability was more need than nature. A need to love, and to be loved.

As a child Dinah already revealed a concern for love. At the age of five, on returning home from a fortnight with her Granny in the Isle of Wight she made this affecting speech: 'It's funny, Daddy. I love it at Freshwater. I love it at home. I love Mummy. I love you. We love ourselves. Where does it all come from, all this love?' That night, Dinah tucked up in bed, Geraldine sought to share with Phillip her pleasure at their daughter's nascent wisdom. 'It's important. Her loving herself,' she said. The father laughed: 'She meant we all love each other. Not ourselves, necessarily.' A nothing remark; nothing compared with far harsher misunderstandings of their long married life; a remark, though, the memory of which came increasingly to symbolise to Geraldine their essential differences. It pained her more and more that her husband failed to appreciate the things which intimately affected her. Why couldn't he understand that the words themselves were immaterial? What mattered were the feelings behind the words. The emotions. While the child Dinah might have meant to say each other, not ourselves, the mere talking like that signified self-loving. Otherwise she would have avoided the subject altogether – like Phillip did; and her sons did; like all men tended to.

Despite her intense need of love there was no denying Dinah's actually outgoing character, for she bubbled with an extravagant sense of social fun. At school Dinah gained a reputation for anarchy, for being one of those sparky-faced girls on whom the severest punishment had negligible effect. Dinah attracted trouble wherever she went. On visiting matches to other schools her reputation travelled ahead, making her the focus of rival ringleaders' attention. Dinah it was – together with her friend Frances Culbertson – who invariably kept the coach waiting for the return journey. Dinah who recited the rudest stanzas in the sing-song. Dinah who sat in a corner of the back seat and slipped her shoulder strap to passing lorry drivers. Dinah who threw the muddy lacrosse boot which landed in the games mistress' lap. (When they banned Dinah from away matches she joined her mother's Keep Fit Class and behaved like an angel.)

Geraldine admired the way her daughter dragged Alastair out of himself and made a man of him; enjoyed watching her son-in-law begin to like himself. It was pure pleasure to see how openly the pair of them admitted their dependency, and placed love at the centre of their world without restricting the development of separate careers – boosting each other's creative independence, in fact. Dinah, who liked expressing love by touch, would rest both hands on Alastair's arm at dinner on Friday nights in Godstow and recount news of his latest success. Geraldine missed their weekend visits. In the confusion, after nine blissful years, of this challenge to Dinah and Alastair's love Geraldine instantly forgave the exaggerated nonsense they talked. The single track insensitivity of Alastair's phone calls and letters, his pompous sentimentality, his repetition of wayward imaginings was accepted by Geraldine as natural in such highly charged times. She did not blame him personally for the pain her daughter suffered.

If anyone she blamed Dinah: for treating Alastair as an emotional cripple and doing his feeling for him. Geraldine blamed Dinah for failing to see that it was time for her patient to feed himself, to get up out of bed and stand on his own two feet. One stage of Dinah's work was complete; time now to move on to the next.

The solidity of Dinah's desire to mother Alastair frightened Geraldine, frightened her on Dinah's own account, on Alastair's and on account of the child she hoped they would one day make together. However great the love felt for another – as mother, lover, daughter – all it was ever possible to do, Geraldine believed, the best anyone could hope to achieve was to release in persons loved the ability to feel for themselves; help them to trust the messages posted in their own hearts. What right had Dinah to imagine herself better qualified than Alastair to interpret how he felt? Dinah was in danger of developing the kind of love from which Geraldine had spent the whole of her post-pubescent life in flight – until death rescued her from the emotional blackmail of her own mother's sacrificial loving. The pressure of being – albeit in witty, inventive, chaotic, joyful celebration – the principal focus of concern in life for her energetic mother was a burden she refused to pass on to Dinah or the boys. You're too much, Mother. Your love is just too much for me: Geraldine had longed to say but had never found the courage so to do, fearing the shock on the old woman's face at her rejection of a lifetime's generosity – knowing too that her own guilt would long outlast the other's distress. 'If you love someone,' Geraldine once heard her mother telling Dinah, 'there is nothing you will not do for them, whatever the cost to yourself. Your hurt is my hurt, my darling girl. What's life for if I can't kiss my grandchild better?'

Alastair and Dinah needed time. Given time they would together find the right way forward: Geraldine continued to be convinced.

In addition to Alastair's pigheadedness, however, there was Dinah's temper to contend with, the threat that her daughter might let rage wreak the kind of damage which can never be repaired. The worst of words, the most poisonous diatribe, the angriest of bitter insults can in time be wiped from memory. Not images though. The passage of a whole life of time cannot expunge the haunting recall of horrors seen: pain on a loved one's face, contorted by spasms of hatred. Geraldine knew this from her personal experience of her War. Nothing had dimmed her working memories of wartime London's pain.

The anguish of memory was worse, she knew, for the men of her generation, the men – boys many of them – who won the war. She saw it in their faces still, in the survivor's grey shadow of unforgetfulness, of non-forgiving. Geraldine saw it every day in her husband Phillip's rubicund features. A picture of well-fed *bonhomie*, of the successful man at peace with himself, acquaintances presumed. Less talkative than might have been expected, perhaps. Duller and dourer in character than in looks. A man, it transpired, with surprisingly little to say for himself. He watched and smiled and poured the drinks but seldom seemed to be really there: the Oxford crowd agreed. So very different from his wife, and their terrific daughter.

On Phillip's return from France Geraldine's initial feeling had been of relief at the miracle of his unblemished survival. It was only when the smile of greeting stayed fixed, frozen, to his features that she began to worry. These worries deepened with his failure in the months following the War's end to hold her in his arms for more than a few minutes without beginning to shake uncontrollably, culminating in a whole night of torment for the poor man. They had given up eventually and taken to their separate bedrooms – where they remained, forty years on. Whilst acknowledging her sorrow, Geraldine never resented this denial of conjugal intimacy, nor sought alternative satisfaction. Neither did she permit herself to feel jealous when she learnt – through her younger son Geoffrey's calculatedly wounding letter – about the tart Phillip visited in Maida Vale. It was Geraldine, in fact, who suggested he spend his City nights with the woman. Footing all the expenses of Sally's bijou lovenest – the friendship, Geraldine discovered, was long established, dating back to before the War – it seemed idiotic to pile up smokescreen bills at his Club as well.

Why? was all she needed to know. Why was Phillip able to

make love to Sally and not to her? Why had he felt obliged to lie? Why, when his heart lay elsewhere, did he stay with her now the children had left home?

Geraldine did not shy from the possibility of Phillip divorcing her – indeed, given her cerebral outlook on life, she accepted the prospect of a challenge. Learning to live without physical affection, without the touch of adult love, learning uncomplainingly to suppress desire had bred in her, over the years, a bold independence of spirit. There were plenty of things she wanted to do – complete her last Open University credit and take her degree, for one; make more time available for her JP's duties, for another. She did not so much mind what Phillip's answers to her questions might be; it was not having them which irked.

Geraldine realised that in giving up the big house she would most have missed the garden she and Phillip had created together out of the wreckage of the War. She would have hated, she knew, losing Fred and Tony, their gardeners, father and son. Saying goodbye to the cleaning ladies and denying them – by closing up the family home in Godstow – the daily focus of their lives would have been difficult too. It was the household she would miss, Geraldine worked out, not the house itself. Although she did not at all mind the idea of no longer being able to host each year's family rituals, and happily envisaged going to her sons' homes instead. They could take their pivotal turns.

And Dinah? Would Dinah and Alastair not be together to be visited too?

Geraldine admired the stylishness with which Alastair and Dinah had converted her friend Fifi Vollmer's stable wing in Blackheath, earning themselves a six-page spread in *House and Garden*. Not only did she like their style better than Christopher's or Geoffrey's, but she also preferred their company. Both her boys – born in quick succession during the early years of the War – laboured under the illusion that life was a trick, into the secret of which they were bound sooner or later to be initiated. Of her daughter she had always held higher hopes – hopes which had promised fulfilment when Dinah stepped out of line to marry Alastair, unperturbed by her father's tight-lipped opposition. It saddened Geraldine to think that it was Dinah's marriage, rather than her own, which was now at risk.

Phillip had never been able to explain his behaviour to his wife. Merely pleaded, repeatedly, 'You are a wonderful woman, Geraldine. A wonderful, wonderful woman.' There could be no comparison, he maintained, between her and Sally; and no question of his leaving her – death alone would divide the family. It proved useless for Geraldine to expect him to talk about his feelings, pointless to press him to explain why he felt and acted as he did – for he found expression of emotion impossible. All the men Geraldine knew were the same. When she asked Christopher once what he felt about a particular girl he was dating he replied: 'I really think she loves me, Mummy.' As if man recognised his feelings for woman solely through knowing hers for him. As if the question of how and what man felt could only be answered by someone else. This was the main reason, Geraldine concluded, for men making more effective politicians than women. Ask a man a question about a particular subject and he either answered the same question about a different subject or a different question about the same subject, whichever was the least revealing. Automatically, without requiring a moment's pause for thought.

The existence of Phillip's love affair accorded with another of Geraldine's pet theories – concerning balance. In her opinion the measure of happiness and sadness meted out over a lifetime was evenly balanced, no individual on the planet ending up better off than any other. Her husband's nights of abandon with Sally were the least he deserved after the horrors of Normandy. Correspondingly, lack of satisfaction in this area of her own life was balanced by an abundance of reward in other fields: the children; their and her impeccable health; her work as a JP; all sorts of exciting things. Some people were never excited about anything, could never think of anything they really wanted to do and therefore never knew true happiness. Such people – Geraldine concluded – were equally incapable of recognising sadness and eked out their time in the bigoted bliss of ignorance, spared her and Dinah's sickening dashes from the pit of despair to the peak of elation, and back again. Her and their final balance sheets, Dinah's too, would all read zero. Nothing in life came free. Every gift – of love, of laughter – had to be paid for.

Marriage was also a matter of balance, the balance of man by woman, gain by loss, joy by sorrow. It was true, Geraldine agreed, what her men all seemed voicelessly to say: that they could fully know themselves only through knowing her.

When would they begin convincingly to try?

It was around about then, I think, when I began to appreciate Kathy's gift to me: of time. If I'd been allowed my way I'd have been living with her within weeks of walking out on Dinah, the relationship doomed from the start. If Kathy had dropped the hint of a desire to see me I'd have been banging at her door, ringing her bell all hours of the night. However far away she now lived – in Manchester I used to think.

I'm no judge of time, or timing. For me it's always the right time: to do what I want. Right for me, and therefore for others, I easily persuade myself. Until recently each successive moment of the day was *the* moment, the very best moment to see Kathy. The moment after might be too late: I used to fear, sick from yearning. I'm glad, now, she did not yield to my pleadings, glad she has the strength to remain true to her own sense of timing.

I've been forcing myself to think about female periods, and have developed a theory that it's this which gives women instinctive knowledge when and how to show their feelings: the secret of womanhood, a gift all men long to hold. I do anyway – though it's a longing I've never before articulated to myself. Women *sense* when the time is right, that's why they're surer of themselves than we men. Kathy is so accurately in tune with herself that she's able to feel what's best for me too. A kind of telepathy: because I'm thinking hard of her she manages to sense the right time for me better than I can for myself, I reckon.

Kathy protects me from myself.

Woman protects man from damaging himself, protects him

from internal danger. Whilst man protects woman from the dangers of the world outside. That's the arrangement.

I wish Kathy would let me play my role, settle my half of the bargain.

It's good she refused to see me during those first months in Highbury Grove. I was in such a feeble state I'd have collapsed, weeping, into her arms; dried my tears in her thick black hair; melted to nothing in the comfort of her caring. I don't want that – I don't want her to feel sorry for me. I need her to admire me, to count on me. I dream of passion, of passionate love-making . . . But I don't want just a week, a month, a year of passion and then over. I want forever.

It's crucial to be at my best when Kathy and I finally come together: so she'll never want to leave. That's why she's waiting: to minimise the risk of my failing her. And she's right, it . . . us, I mean, she-and-me, we two are too important to take risks with.

'Give it time, Alastair.' I used to think this meant it was she who needed time. I see now it's me Kathy is thinking of, not herself.

It's all a question of balance, isn't it?

As well as needing to feel in control, I also want to let go. I long to forget myself in the physical passion of being with Kathy. To exist totally in a world bounded by us two, a world without dimension beyond the touch of our two skins. Nothing else. To feel nothing else but her; to lose myself in her – in her smells, her sounds, her touches, her looks, her breaths. To bury myself deep inside her; so deep that I become her.

All these contradictions. I'm getting confused again.

You see, I'm also afraid of losing myself. Terrified. It's bad enough on my own. Sitting quietly here alone, I locate an essential bit of me when . . . Puff! . . . and it's gone, lost, disappeared, maybe never to return. How much more tenuous is my hold on myself likely to be within the pull of Kathy's presence?

I've learnt an amazing amount through Kathy's gift to me of time, things I needed to discover on my own to be of any use to anyone else. There seems no end to the things in life I should have known about, should have discovered years ago.

I get the latest discovery straight in my head and prepare myself for seeing Kathy, then something else crops up; I find another key piece of the jigsaw hidden beneath the carpet. I used to be sure I was ready for her at any moment. Now I'm worried I might never be.

Drink, and cigarettes; I still haven't conquered drink. A whole bottle of wine last night here on my own after returning barely sober from supper with the Hawthorns. So childish. Today I can't remember a word of those vital decisions I made last night; can't reach the feelings poured despairingly into drunken tears. Heaviness, tiredness, uselessness: they're all that remain.

Better go to bed.

Nine-fifteen and I'm retreating to bed?

I don't deserve her.

If Kathy were already mine I might be less confident of my affinity with other women. If last year Kathy and I had come together I might never have discovered the depth – and breadth – of my sympathy for women in general. I might have been open only to her, unaware of the lovingness of others; insensitive to the needs of all women; ignorant of their need to trust in me, and of my capacity to respond.

Because of the intensity of my own feelings there were times when I probably went over the top in my mission to heal (the thought of an attempt to console Eleanor de Rougemont makes my flesh creep). Frances, I know, is critical. She says it's not my sensitivity to their needs, but theirs to mine. But I know Frances is wrong. She's jealous, disillusioned by her own broken affairs, the trail of destruction in her own wake.

It was Sandra Poole – funny little Sandra, of all people – who first alerted me to my fundamental attractiveness to women. At dinner, a reward for working late with me at Roxeth House, she said something so nice about Kathy that I squeezed her hand. Sandra didn't stop there, but went on to tell me how much she admired my tenderness – life-enhancing: she said it was. In saying she thought Kathy may have found my love too much to take in all at once, Sandra was speaking secretly for herself.

I made Sandra promise to say straight out, without fear for the hurt to me, if she had reason to suspect Kathy wouldn't be coming back.

She hasn't said anything yet.

Sandra Poole believes Kathy will be unable to resist in the end. And she knows more of what happened between us than anyone. From her secretarial desk in the office Sandra witnessed my brushing with my hand the lock of hair from Kathy's face. Sandra knows how much Kathy looked forward to seeing me; knows how wide Kathy opened her eyes to smile at me; knows the delight of our work together on the Appeal; knows the girl loved – loves – me.

Women have always been drawn to me. I was too naive, till recently, to respond properly. That's what it is.

Think of Penny, the teacher I met when I was in Doncaster, working as a labourer on the by-pass to earn my university money after Dad refused to pay his share.

Penny almost thirty, married, the mother of two; me, only nineteen, a virgin. 'Look Cilla,' she once said to a friend, the three of us standing in her kitchen waiting for the kettle to boil. 'See how he kisses.' And she kissed me – mouth open, belly pressing. 'There. He'll kiss you if you want. Won't you Al?' Laughing, Cilla stepped up for her go.

Penny invited me to their New Year's Eve party: she and her husband Timothy – a teacher too, at the same school – Cilla and her husband Jim, three other Doncaster couples, and me. I enjoyed it. The women played around with each other's husbands – nothing serious: smooching to the record player; a bit of petting on the floor. Penny ended up on my knee in a chair by the fire. Her lightness surprised me: like a girl, not a mother. I remember admiring her long fingernails – false, she said – beautiful red hair and almost transparent skin. 'You're not bad yourself,' she told me. 'Might give you a kiss.'

After that first time we kissed a lot, mostly in the evenings, lying full length on the sofa, Timothy snoring in bed upstairs. 'Serves him right,' Penny used to say – I never knew for what. Before I left for my summer in the South of France we arranged to meet down in London for a farewell lunch; at Chez Victor in Wardour Street, the only Soho restaurant I knew then – *Le patron mange ici* inscribed on the window. Penny wore crimson stiletto heels and a light grey twopiece. We went back to her sister's flat for tea. Her sister was out at work, but Penny had the key: not a flat, it turned out, but a ground floor bedsitter in South Kensington, the room taller than it was wide. Penny said her blouse and tights were sweaty, needed a wash.

I'd never seen her bare shoulders – except at the swimming pool.

We kissed as usual.

I suppose she expected me to make love to her. I can't imagine – now – why I didn't. I don't remember thinking of it at the time. It never occurred to me that I should; or could, probably.

Actually, thinking back again, I'm almost sure I didn't want to 'do' it. Because it felt . . . well, sort of dirty. Her being married, and older than me.

That's it, I remember now. At the swimming pool, with her and the kids one Sunday afternoon, I saw pubic hairs poking out of her bikini. I hated that, I really did. Dark red hairs, darker than her head, curling out against the white of her scrawny thighs.

So blatant.

So basic.

I still don't understand how a man can kiss a woman there. Or how she can let him. It's disgusting. Like animals. Dogs licking arses in the gutter.

Wrong of me, I dare say. Probably missing out. It might've been better if I'd let Penny have her way with me, let her teach me how to kiss a woman between the legs.

I loved kissing Penny's lips – the plucking and sucking and pressing, and the long reach of her tongue up beneath my gums.

She wouldn't allow me to take a photo of her, so I pinched a set of her false nails instead. Kept them for ages at the back of the drawer in my bedside cupboard.

Nineteen and still a virgin – five years later I was grown-up enough to marry?

Despite their violence, I can't help but respect those letters of Dinah's. Her love last year switched to hate. Everything I said or wrote was wrong, every tearful attempt at explanation. When I came, finally, to acknowledge Kathy's part in it all that too was wrong.

If I took the blame upon myself I was denying Dinah's existence as an individual, treating her as an inanimate object – apparently. When I spoke of viewing her essentially as a family person and myself as a loner I negated her achievements as an artist, insulted her struggle for self-expression.

Dinah laid waste to everything about me. *As for your parents' hypocritical, pathetic marriage which has made you what you are. . . .*

She knows how to be unkind, I'll grant her that.

I tried to tell her I was sure she'd make a success of things without me to weigh her down.

A success of what? Of being a well-used lover? A whore? Since love doesn't and never did exist. Instead of telling me how marvellous I am tell me all the horrible characteristics in me you absolutely loathe and cannot stand to be with any longer. As for me, from now onwards I'll dedicate my life to cleansing my guts of you. I won't rest until every smile, every laugh, every kiss of yours has been vomited up and flushed away. Even if it takes the rest of my life.

Dinah, not me, initiated the separation proceedings: in a crisp letter from my own solicitor – accompanied by a handwritten note expressing his personal regret at the firm being unable, due to the conflict of interests, to act on my behalf as well. After all our promises to make whatever decisions became necessary together, to continue to do whatever *we* thought was best, regardless of expert advice, she let herself sink to a lawyer's ugly letter: documenting every penny her parents had given us over the years; listing which wedding presents came from her side of the family; demanding sole ownership of the house and studio, and offering me the car, the hi-fi system and the Marks and Spencer shares. No financial obligations thereafter on either side.

I've no grounds for complaint, I know. I'm not complaining. It's what I want.

Can it be? I'm not sure anyone in their right mind could actually want this to happen.

I'm being stupid. It's the same for everyone. There's nothing special about us, our break-up is no more tragic than anybody else's.

Bitter coldness after such warmth, the cold hard division of assets – as if 'assets' is all they are. Our car isn't just any car: it's where you sang to me on Sunday night drives home from Oxford to Blackheath; it's where you dropped a triple ice cream cone down your front; it's where you told me you weren't pregnant after all.

I don't think I'll ever have the energy to make another home. All the papering and painting and picture-hanging; sanding, staining, sealing; deciding colours; choosing mattresses. I'll live in other people's houses, sleep in someone else's bed.

My lawyer (Belinda's lawyer) instructs me that as Dinah is childless and has ample means of self-support a division of seventy/thirty – seventy per cent of our joint assets to me – is all the law requires. When I insist that everything be equally divided, and explain that this is the basis on which we've always conducted our marriage, the lawyer drops her professional guard and becomes quite human. The law's wrong: she said the other day. You're not being generous, you're being fair: she said.

The lawyer likes me.

She thinks Dinah will change her mind at the last moment and ask me back – and that I'll go.

Ever since Dinah decided to make our separation official I've been revisited by childhood nightmares. My sleep is regularly shattered by images of elephantiasis: of Kathy's legs, Susannah's legs, every woman's legs swollen to giant awfulness. Women hobble down Shaftesbury Avenue on great pustular treetrunks – beneath the bedclothes my own grotesque legs are dead to my touch. Another vision: a swarm of locusts flies in through the bedroom window. I dive for cover beneath the blankets and hear the remorseless beat of the locusts' wings against the eiderdown. In the silence which follows I emerge, switch on the light, and find I'm blind.

Happier memories are beginning to recur alongside the nightmares. Of playing conkers at Oakdene. I was good at conkers, knew which to choose, what skewer to use and where and how to strike – the way you strike makes all the difference. I developed a plunging sideways swoop, catching the rival conker as close as possible to the string. One year I had a two hundred and eighty niner, the school record. A bigger boy, at least a head taller – lock forward in our Prep School fifteen – claimed I'd cheated. I rushed at him full tilt and knocked him to the ground. It was wet, I remember, as we rolled around on the reddish gravel of the yard. I got a cut lip – but wouldn't give in, and it was he who called pax in the end.

I can't get over how supportive Sarah-Jane has been. Uncritically, uninquisitively supportive, never telling me how I should – or shouldn't – feel. Not wanting to add to my burden, she remains undisturbed in herself at my distress.

I wish she lived closer in to town.

I wish I could speak to her now, instead of talking to myself.

It was Dinah's fault that I lost touch with Sarah-Jane. Dinah disliked my sister from the beginning. Said she was selfish. Said she neglected my mother. Dinah claims she did twice as much as Sarah-Jane to entertain my parents. It's true: Dinah was lovely with my mother, increased the sum of Mum's happiness a hundredfold. No reason, though, to take it out on Sarah-Jane. It's different for her: she's Mum's daughter.

When Sarah-Jane walked out on Bob I castigated her for not loving him enough. Dinah and I would give up everything to preserve our marriage; we put love above everything: I remember telling her. I'm afraid I'd caught Dinah's bad opinion of my sister and didn't stop to think how awful she must have been feeling; nor how courageous it was of her to admit, after eighteen months of marriage, she had picked the wrong man. It's us, Dinah and I, who were the self-centred ones, ordering the universe around our sacred togetherness. What price 'us' now?

It's unfair of me to blame Dinah exclusively for my loss of contact with Sarah-Jane. We first lost contact years before – when I was eight years old, and started at Oakdene.

Sarah-Jane and I had been such friends till I went to Prep School and deserted her for boys, forming a special gang – Charlie, me and Jonty – and forgetting about my sister. By the time the gang split up and I needed her again she was unavailable, locked into her girl's world.

Girls destroyed the gang. Girls – I now realise – became my enemy. Boys are forced to consort with girls, are driven to accommodate them while remaining forever – until now? – the enemy.

Yes, it'll be different now. It'll be how I've in the past pretended it was – only this time it'll be for real, not a performance.

I can see, as if it were yesterday, Charlie and Judith's gumboots poking out from a hideout we'd built amongst the bales of straw in Jonty's father's barn. I was flabbergasted. Didn't know what to do. Was about to shout: 'Hey! What's going on?' and tug at their coupled legs . . . but didn't. I slipped home on my bicycle. Soon afterwards Judith was made an official member of our gang, and brought a friend along for Jonty. The girls took to teasing me. And the boys allowed them to: that's what hurt. It was Charlie's wholesale desertion to the enemy which I found so difficult to take.

The same year my Headmaster at Oakdene also let me down – by the feebleness of his leavers lecture. I'd got it into my head that the HM's man-to-man chat with school leavers would explain everything – I mean: about how to deal with girls, be friends with the opposite sex. In the end he talked awesomely about mothers and not at all about girls. The only subject touched upon in any detail was the euphemistic 'tendency' of older boys at boarding school. He – like my father – managed to make boys sound even more dangerous than girls, and I left for Hillhead in some confusion.

Being chosen to play Queen of the Faeries in *A Midsummer Night's Dream* during my second term as a boarder didn't help. I can laugh about it now, but at the time I took the responsibility in deadly earnest. I liked playing Titania, in fact, was flattered at being selected for the part.

I wasn't embarrassed at portraying a woman – the make-up and false boobs made me feel grown-up, the handling of such matters more man's business than boy's. My dress was green and silver, with a bustle and ruff, a string of plastic pearls (poppers, I think they were called) festooning my grey-green wig. I felt regal – distinctly superior to Hippolyte, a tall day-boarder who looked more like a girl dressed up as a boy than the other way round. 'Ill met by moonlight, proud Titania,' Oberon greeted my first entrance. Playing it haughty, I pretended I hadn't seen or heard him; except, if he was a second late on cue, I spoilt the effect by glaring in his supposedly hidden direction. 'What jealous Oberon? Faeries skip hence. I have foresworn his bed and company . . .' I was okay until reaching the speech about a pregnant black maid, her belly swelling like a sail. The English master urged me to communicate the Queen's secret pride at her Oberon's virility, a pride cloaked in outward anger at his unfaithfulness. It was all a bit much for me.

Auntie Phyllis (my godmother) adored me as Titania. She said I was the spit image of my mother during the War, ordering the fairies around like Mum had the young air crews.

Shakespeare productions at Hillhead are taken seriously all over Yorkshire – the *Post*'s reviewer wrote: 'The uncompromising maleness of the fairies was most refreshing'. The school players were treated with respect not ridicule. Seniors knew my name, chose me to make up fours with them at table tennis – the only ball-game I've ever been any good at – and to run their errands. Nothing happened; nothing was suggested. Except by the Housemaster, who accused me of seducing the Captain of Rugger. When I protested my innocence he wagged a forefinger at me: 'There's no smoke without fire, Shore. You're a nasty little flirt.'

The Captain of Rugger takes a shine to Titania and it's the thirteen year old's fault? Maybe I was a trifle over-charming, but it was fun – and nothing happened. I thought he was great, actually; Hillhead's best fly-half in years.

The fragility of life astonishes me. I used to think people were defeated by their own weaknesses, that only weak people let life defeat them. Life is fair: I used to think. Life isn't, life is by definition unfair – to everyone. No one escapes.

Look at Miss Gaydon, Games Mistress for thirty years at Moores's in Dulwich, moving spirit of the Merton Hockey Festival, a fixed star in the firmament for hundreds of her favourite pupils. And look at her now: bowed and benumbed, rotting in Roxeth House.

'You do it. And it's done.'

Five months after retirement Miss Gaydon jumped hastily down from a bus on her short fat legs and twisted an ankle. Confined day and night to her flat for the first time in her life, Miss Gaydon disintegrated; her joints swelled, her head drooped and the once-ebullient hockey fanatic was transformed within a matter of weeks into a wheelchair invalid. The accident occurred shortly before Christmas, and Miss Gaydon refused to open any of her cards. Meaningless, she apparently said they were. 'What am I to them now?'

When we agreed to take Miss Gaydon in at Roxeth House she was so ill she couldn't read a word. No newspapers, nothing. She usen't to be able to watch television even.

Maybe Miss Gaydon never stopped to think till it was too late? Immobilised in her flat maybe it dawned on her she had the whole thing wrong, that she had prepared hundreds of girls over the years for a world which doesn't exist. Maybe the inexperienced old maid's faith in society vanished – and with this loss her entire world crumbled, her being disintegrated.

Breakdown is a form of anger, two sides of the same coin. Miss Gaydon is furious with herself for getting life wrong.

I've never seen my mother break down and cry – but I've certainly seen her angry. About the angriest I've seen her was when my father allowed a goat to brush against her favourite green skirt. I was seven, I should think. We were on holiday in Scotland, on a farm, and this scraggy old goat kept following Mum around. She tried to shoo him away, explaining to us that the stink of goats on clothes was ineradicable. When my father's attempts at protection proved worthless and the goat succeeded in rubbing himself against her, Mum was absolutely furious.

It sounds like a Freudian dream I know. It isn't though.

I've a feeling Dinah is more annoyed with herself than with me. She won't accept a word against me from anyone else, however vicious she herself might be. What right have they to criticise? she says. She says I'm twice the man of any husband of theirs.

You're twice the woman, my love.

My love? Still?

Always my love.

Dinah's anger has given me the worst moment of my life: last year, on an ordinary autumn morning. I'd arranged an interview with Sir Ralph Janson, the greatest living British architect – in my opinion: I rate his reviled Ministry of Defence a masterpiece. We'd been talking for about three quarters of an hour when the phone on his desk rang. Sir Ralph, who had instructed his secretary not to put through any calls, began a sharp rebuttal – then stopped, handed me the receiver. 'It's for you. Sorry,' he said.

I thought Dinah had killed Kathy. I did. That was my instinctive reaction.

Shauna Greenstock – one of our picture researchers – wanted me to return immediately to the office where Dinah had barged in and started wrecking the place. A security guard had been forced physically to restrain her. She had quietened down, Shauna told me, but refused to leave until she'd seen me. 'My wife. She's in trouble. I'll have to go,' I mumbled at Sir Ralph.

I found Dinah on the floor amongst the debris of my office. Crumpled in the corner. Like a rag doll. She was drumming her head against the partition, just below the level of the glass, muttering untouchably to herself. I knelt on the floor in front of her and took her hand. The hand was cold, her eyes expressionless, dead to the outside world. 'Come back. Come back, my love,' I pleaded. (I was afraid she'd fallen over the edge into the abyss.) 'Come back, please come back, my love. My love,' I continued – very softly, seeking gently to break the rhythm of her wordless chant.

Tears welled, then poured down her face, and she pressed my hand to her cheek.

On the drive home to Blackheath she explained that a letter from my solicitor had triggered the storm. She hadn't planned harm: she promised. Had simply needed – desperately – to see me, been desperate for contact to dispel the emptiness inside. She'd been willing to wait, but then something happened in her head; a switch clicked and she went berserk, consumed by a blind desire to destroy me and everything connected to me.

It wouldn't recur: she said. She couldn't risk the humiliation.

Shortly before I left her that morning she made a strange remark about Kathy. She told me she'd seen Kathy again and that the girl reminded her of herself when we first met. It seems Dinah believes I've fallen in love with the image of herself as she once was. She says my loving Kathy is like wanting to start all over again with her, but as this isn't possible it's got to be with someone else.

How can she think that when they're so different?

Dinah said she hoped Kathy would change her mind and agree to see me. She says she hopes I'll find happiness with Kathy.

I'm more confident these days that Dinah will reach the other side without loss of spirit.

Although the memory of her slumped in the corner of my office never leaves me – thrown there by me, by my desertion of our love.

I've had to change offices. To one in which the desk faces a window and my chair can be wedged against the back and side walls, leaving no space spare for the hauntings.

Frances Culbertson took Alastair to bed out of curiosity, to test for herself the gaucheness Dinah often complained about. Friends since schooldays in Oxford, Frances and Dinah had shared for years their dreams and disappointments, each suspecting the other of exaggeration, of competing to impress. Frances doubted Dinah's experiences with men had ever been as good – or bad – as she claimed. Sex, Frances suspected, was no less of a problem for Dinah than she made it out to be for Alastair.

'It's the quality of feeling which counts. Women seem to sense my caring before I'm aware of it myself. I'd never noticed this before. Everything was always us. Dinah-and-me. Me-and-Dinah. I never noticed others' needs.' Alastair took a swig of wine, wiped a dribble from his combative chin and lay back in one of the paisley-covered armchairs in Frances' conventionally comfortable living room. 'Women all over London are crying out for a touch of gentleness. Of attention. They are. I know you think I'm naive. I tell you they are, though.'

Frances frowned: to save herself laughing.

'Admit it. It's the truth. Look at your record. How you manage to pick up so many prize shits I've no idea. Maybe you're a masochist?'

'And you're the expert soother?'

'It's got nothing to do with expertise. Sex isn't a skill, you know. It's feelings. Touch. Things like that. Technique's a red herring. Bloody manuals. Some publisher minting money, that's all. The Karma Sutra? Leave that to schoolboys.'

After the worthlessness of his words Alastair's physical quality in bed took Frances by surprise, his skin warm and soft, the flesh beneath reassuringly solid. He lay on top of her and kissed her lips, eyes, ears, the whole of her face with a delicate precision, pressing the weight of his body steadily down between her legs. Relaxing to his attractiveness, Frances came as effortlessly as she ever remembered – although Alastair appeared barely to notice her pleasured chuckle: 'How about that!' and continued his self-absorbed routine. Once fully erect he gave her tits a token slobber and offered her his cock. Frances gathered she was expected to manoeuvre herself into position for him to make an entry – which she did – and he worked himself off inoffensively enough. Frances smiled in the dark. Sex with her best friend's husband had proved surprisingly nice, not invasive at all – more a harbouring. Frances liked the feeling left behind from Alastair's love-making, more tender than of passion spent or sex satiated. A sense of having given rather than been taken.

In the morning, when Frances settled to present his sleepy body with a thank-you treat, she was disappointed to feel Alastair grow tense the lower her tongue explored. When she reached his tummy-button he grabbed her shoulders and hauled her back up the bed, rolling over on top of her in attempted replay of the night's performance.

'Sorry.'

'Not at all. You're lovely just to be with. Such beautiful skin. For a man.'

'It's you who's beautiful,' Alastair countered.

Frances snuggled her head into her favoured resting place, between a partner's chin and collar-bone. She knew how she looked naked in the morning: flesh yellow, eyes bagged and black, hair lifelessly disordered, breasts and belly no longer young. Yet, in a funny way, she felt Alastair meant what he said, and was moved by his saying it.

Afterwards, knowing they were unlikely ever again to be intimate, Frances regretted not having explained to him that few women reach orgasm through penetration – or feel anything much at all, in fact. She regretted not having attempted to make Alastair understand it was his tenderness which mattered, his lightness of touch which had given her as much pleasure as anything she had experienced with a man.

Whilst appreciative of Alastair's tenderness, Frances was infuriated by his sentimentality. By the way he bored on about his 'young love' for Kathy Abraham, proclaiming blind faith in love's power to sustain the absent object of affection. By the way he constantly reiterated his fears for Dinah's safety without mention of his own agony. By the way he romanticised truth: 'must be *true* to myself'; 'can't *truly* say I love her any longer'; 'only going to write the *truth* from now on' . . . and other such nonsense, unworthy of intelligent attention. Alastair kidded himself he was playing the truth game when all he was actually doing, Frances informed him, was being foolish. As soon as his marriage demanded a little effort, what did he do? Gave up, retreated into the fantasy of 'togetherness' – but with somebody else.

Marriage was insane. Couples entered central commitments, made life-altering contracts without sensible consideration for a single month ahead, much less for the long years of lonely incompatibility. And with marriage came children. Why did so many otherwise practical women – who regularly confronted their own disappointments in men – perpetuate in their children false hopes of fulfilment in coupledom? Surely they knew that no one else could be the solution. Frances quoted Christa Wolf at Alastair: 'To become oneself, with all one's strength. Difficult.' Impossible: she warned him, if he let himself depend on Kathy.

Having more or less given up on men in the Seventies, women in the Eighties were the greater sadness to Frances – educated women especially, who ought to be braver. Frances despised women whose response to their discovery of life's imbalances was to capitulate to motherhood. It was every woman's duty to satisfy her intimate self, not to use children as an excuse, a bulwark between her and self-determination. Protect her children? What for? For them to follow her lead into frustrated unfulfilment? Motherly conversation overhead in the park drove Frances mad: about little Will being such a bad eater, and young Paul's temper, and baby Sal sleeping so poorly – the pointless toil of a mother, geriatric enjoyment of grandchildren her distant goal. Frances once slapped a stranger in the face (near the round pond in Kensington Gardens). 'Oh dear, Tommy,' the mother was saying, staring in depressive resentment at her child. 'What in the world have I done to deserve you?' Was the child guilty from birth of being a burden to his mother? 'I'll kick your teeth down your throat,' Frances overheard – in the Underground – a woman shout at another boy, the woman's body fat and fearsome, the child's bewildered eyes gazing into the distance. Or was it better to grow up unloved but free from guilt than badly loved and forever burdened?

Frances reckoned the English were the most sentimental race on earth, champion armchair hand-wringers at 'national tragedies': the sinking of the Sir Galahad in the Falklands War, for example – not a tear for the Argentinians, it was worth remembering. And what about the Iran Air passenger plane US-missiled from the sky above the Persian – Persian note, not American – Gulf? Frances' random recall turned to the destruction of a Welsh mining village beneath an unstable slag heap, to irredeemable images of parents scrabbling in the black earth to reach their children buried at school. People mourned the tragedy of Aberfan, a celluloid pit village, and ignored equal injustice in their own streets, preferred not to see the day-to-day awfulness of individual experience within the family's bosom. What about the fact that for some of those children in Aberfan death was an escape, escape from the insufferable violence of their fathers, violence which in many cases would have been repeated by their husbands?

Justice, justice in life mattered, not life *per se*. The preservation of terminally deprived, defiled, despoiled life, of permanently dismayed and disappointed life for life's sentimental sake made no sense.

Frances attached no greater value to her own life than to anybody else's – less, in fact. She took risks – put herself about (Frances' mildly ironic term for taking sex when and where she needed it, from whoever happened to be around). The rewards were worth the risk, not merely in the sensual enjoyment of basic physical need – sex as pissing rather than sex as therapy (bugger love) – but also in the satisfaction of feeling in control, of exercising her right to choose. Sure, there were side effects: a certain loneliness in the ritual exchange of hang-dog partners; her tendency to drink at night, not eat; the discovery that autonomy – power over self, in other words – was not the same as control. On occasion Frances was tempted to conclude that she paid too high an annual fee for so-termed freedom, that the women's liberation movement was a delusion. With all her vaunted independence – authoritative job, public respect, plenty of money – she still relied on men, still let herself be hurt by men.

One relationship particularly disturbed her: with Bill Travis, a property developer. She understood how their friendship suited him, but what did it do for her? Why did she tolerate, year after year, its incurable fallibility? The locked-in feeling frightened Frances, made her vaguely aware that she might one night be forced to murder him as the only means of release. She had tried other methods: like damaging his prized motor car. Driving him back to her flat after dinner – Bill always made her drive when they were over the limit – she had scraped the Jensen from bumper to bumper down the side of a builder's skip, and burst into hoots of laughter. 'If you don't shut up I'll dump you right here,' he had threatened. 'Good!' she had replied. Chuckling to herself she had wandered off down the street, delighted to have seen the last of Bill Travis.

Three months later, late at night, he was back knocking at her door – and she let him in. Unable to say no, unwilling to say yes, she slipped back into the same age-old routine of sexual submission. Bill Travis knew exactly what he wanted and she let him take it, whenever he wished – the more it hurt, some nights, the better. Even at times when her head told her it could not be right, Frances' body enjoyed the way they screwed.

Afterwards, when he had finished with her, Bill would lie back on her bed and in seconds fall asleep. How many times in the five years since they first had sex had she lain beside him, unable to sleep, waiting for him to wake, stretch and leave?

In the early days she had lain as if asleep, her arms folded about him, legs enmeshed, praying that for once he would stay all night. She had admired his strength then, but had prayed for him to weaken, to give in to his need to be loved.

She still pretended at the time of parting to be asleep. Still waited anxiously. Still prayed.

Prayed now though for him to bestir himself, retrieve his clothes and return to his own flat. As soon as she heard the front door bang, instead of crying herself to sleep, these days she got up to run a bath, and often sat reading late into the night.

These days Frances thought of herself not of him. Promised herself never to succumb to his power, always to retain some unsoiled part of herself as her own. Frances promised to find the strength to refuse Bill when he asked her – as she knew he would in the end – to marry him.

After her night with Alastair, Frances sent him a quotation from Rilke.

Things are not so comprehensible and expressible as one

would mostly have us believe; most events are inexpressible, taking place in a realm which no word has ever entered . . . Be patient towards all that is unsolved in your heart and try to love the questions themselves. Do not now seek the answers . . . the point is to live everything. Live the questions now . . . Everything that happens keeps on being and beginning.

Frances far from agreed with the whole of this quotation, but it fitted Alastair's mood: she felt. She was pleased to find Alastair asking himself long overdue questions – if only he would ask freely, without pre-fixing the required answers firmly in his mind. His rigid structure of expectation led Frances to doubt Alastair's capacity to appreciate the essence of anybody. He ploughed on about love as though it was a commodity, a matter of his finding in himself 'true' love and bestowing it on the chosen woman for life's problems to be resolved. It never occurred to him that the woman of his choice might disdain such crushing declarations of love, might not share his fantasy of the future, his growth-denying freedom-snuffing ideal of inevitable togetherness. What about woman's own peculiar needs? Did he not realise that a woman had needs of her own, distinct from a man's? Time he found out. Time he gave some thought to how a woman felt for and in herself, regardless of him. Time he assimilated the significance of man being the son of woman, born into the world on a river of female blood.

The contradictions in all this puzzled Frances – the fact that she had no difficulty seeing the way forward for Alastair in such matters, but was incapable of sorting things out for herself. On the rare evenings she spent at home on her own – yearnings for Bill Travis diffused in a fug of claret – Frances' feelings were free to travel down other paths. Embedded in the goose-down cushions of an armchair, legs folded beneath her, she resurrected the longings of a decade earlier and allowed revive her desire to meet a man who made more than mere fashionable response to the challenge of the Women's Movement. A man who could properly let himself go without counting on her to succour him, without fearing change, conflict and confusion. A man open to losing – and to finding – himself. A man secure enough in the unity of his own thought, feeling and action to grant her the freedom to be and become whoever she was. A man who would help her make herself up as she went along – for always.

Then Frances would shake her befuddled head, close her tired eyes, knowing she longed for something which could never happen. Knowing this would never happen because it already had: she had already met this man, had grown to love him and he her – and still it hadn't worked. She had wanted from him both commitment and freedom, to be held and at the same time let go; she had wanted him to love her with passion and with patience; had wanted him never to leave her yet never to need her. And he had wanted all these things of her too. Yet still it hadn't worked. Frances had felt trapped by the very qualities she craved for in a man, drained by him of her essential energies. Drained by love, by the seemingly predestined certainty of his love for her and by the knowledge that whatever plans they laid to combat dependence he would be powerless to prevent her loss of self. Sensing so strongly this danger she had first denied him space and finally cut herself free.

Free to do what? To punish herself with a Bill Travis?

Forever? Was there no going back, no re-beginning?

In Frances' opinion Alastair's ineptitude was not the sole reason for the breakdown of his marriage. Dinah was also at fault – notably in her ruthless manipulation of Alastair in order to jettison her family.

In principle Frances was wholly supportive of Dinah's desire to flee a home controlled by her two hearty brothers and a father the sight of whom had always made Frances squirm (with his health-club suntan, his podgy hands protected for gardening by rubber gloves and his slicked grey hair). As boys Christopher and Geoffrey had been harmless fun, useful for their enthusiasm with the punt pole and as Saturday night chauffeurs. Life for the Pollard boys peaked at twenty and from there descended to a less and less jolly romp through early fatherhood to an empty middle age, hard-nosed pride in family name the main criterion for their decision-making – increasingly intolerant of independent thought of any colour from their wives. Frances continued to receive the occasional *At Home* invitation from *Mrs Christopher Pollard* . . . If Bill Travis could be contracted to call himself Mr Frances Culbertson marriage might almost be worth it! Geoffrey was the meanest. Geoffrey consistently referred to Dinah's weaving as needlework: not because he knew no better but because he enjoyed insulting his sister, relished her belittlement.

Frances noticed early on how Alastair coveted the Pollard family aura. She saw the dangers already at the wedding – and pointed them out, rather drunkenly, to Dinah's busy mother. At their going away – wearing matching blue capes – Frances refused to catch Dinah's bouquet, letting it fall to the gravel.

A sad fact which Frances observed with the passing years was the manner in which Dinah persuaded Alastair to sever his own family ties and take on hers instead. A damagingly contradictory desire: for Alastair to cherish the very things she wished to be rescued from. Frances cringed to see unpompous Alastair adopt his Pollard brothers-in-laws' patrician airs. Enviably loving though Dinah and Alastair became, and fun though it was to share in their celebrations, the emphasis all the time on themselves grew ugly. Everything they touched they had to own: *our* Blackheath, *our* Covent Garden, *our* friends. Frances began to feel like one of their possessions, a pet animal famed for her misdemeanours. It became impossible to disagree with them about anything without being accused of treachery. Discussion ceased, permissible shades of opinion reduced to two: black or white, for or against. With Covent Garden converted to a wilderness of middle-class affluence – fruit warehouses to architects' offices, paint factories to photographic studios, rope makers' yards to country crafts parlours – would they not now admit to the failure of their whole poxy preservation argument? Would they not agree that Alastair's appropriation of the area for the Sunday newspapers had reduced the indigenous community to a cast of 'characters', cardboard cut-outs of real people?

Frances loathed the way families like the Pollards presumed that everybody else's needs were identical to theirs. She hoped that in leaving Dinah, Alastair might unlearn the worst of his Pollard habits; might cease to impose his concerns, his values, his beliefs – however deeply held – on others. Frances hoped Alastair might come to realise that until he made room for others people's feelings in his own heart there could be no place for his in theirs.

I've talked a lot to friends about Dinah. Not for myself – I never feel I'm doing it for myself, more for them: to placate others for the shock of our parting. I've done all that now, given everyone involved all the help I can, honoured my obligations. Got to work out what it means to me.

The thought of becoming free to concentrate on myself brings with it the possibility of peace – a chink of light at a curtained window. I'm outside in the dark, still roaming the streets, peering through privet hedges at lighted windows. I couldn't tell you what peace looks like, not yet; but at least I know it's there, that it exists.

I left Mum till the end. Not sure why. Maybe for fear of her disappointment – perhaps I felt I'd let her down by deserting Dinah. I wrote to her of course, and promised to come up and stay as soon as I could – but I didn't go, not for longer than the odd day or two, till last September. It was an important visit. Presenting Mum with proof of my survival – more than survival, with a guarantee of a future I could securely call my own – released in me the possibility of peace-with-passion which I feel today.

Mum was her usual self: baked my favourite fruit cake, and asked no questions. I was my usual self too: gracelessly ungrateful, irritating no doubt (irritated certainly). Why do I charm the socks off strangers and act the brat with my parents? You'd imagine nothing could be easier than being nice to my mother.

I'm not nice to her. I intend to be, want to be, but never seem to manage it. Not to her satisfaction.

I'd have told her everything if she'd only asked.

Gran never stops asking questions – and waits impatiently for the reply, barely listening, before hitting back with her own thoughts on the subject. Sex is Gran's preferred topic of conversation ('bedroom stuff', she calls it, not sex). For years I squirmed at my Yorkshire grandmother's inquisition: 'Got yourself a girlfriend, Ali boy? No time like the present. Me and your Grandad were courting at sixteen.' My Grandfather died before I was born. Gran has worn black ever since, her bent body elegantly encased in layers of blackness, grey head angled forward, grizzled chin upheld. The precise physical connection between Gran, my father and me escaped teenage comprehension. It's somewhat bewildering to me still. I feel unlike Dad, look unlike Gran, whilst the two of them are different from each other in every observable way.

But I love Gran. She knows more about me than anyone else in the world, now Dinah's gone. (Except Wilf.)

I love Gran enough to disagree with her. Walking her along the North Bay promenade one afternoon – years ago – she'd been pressing me so hard about girlfriends I snapped back. 'Don't much like girls, as a matter of fact.' Gran cackled gleefully: 'Haven't met the right one. Bowl you right over when you do.'

Gran was the person I first told about Dinah. The two of us were staying on our own in a hotel at Rosedale Abbey, in the middle of the moors (my turn at holiday escort: part duty, part fun). Gran was in such endearingly high spirits at dinner on our first evening I couldn't resist sharing with her my discovery of love. She examined me over the rim of her wine glass: 'Don't let the girl fancy she has it all her own way, will you? See she knows there's others in the offing. I always did. Had dozens of men in the offing in my time. One of them was a policeman. Your Grandad was most put out!' Tipsy after half a bottle of wine at dinner and two sherries before, Gran crawled up the stairs to bed on her hands and knees. 'Better to be safe and silly than sorry in hospital,' she stopped half way up the stairs to explain, oblivious to public ridicule.

It was sad to see her last September, laid so low. I felt I was saying goodbye to her, and to the familiar flat, to the scent of her rosewood wardrobe of beautiful black dresses. I said cheerio to Scarborough too. Can't imagine I'll go back to Gran's beloved 'Scar' without her being there.

I slept on the divan in the sitting room (a nurse was in the spare bedroom) and read Proust beneath the mellow light of a lace-frilled standard lamp. *Remembrance of Things Past*, a birthday present from Dinah, two only of the three volumes for some reason. (She sends presents to hurt now, not to please. Why can't she leave me alone?) I swam first thing every morning in the big public pool, masquerading as a regular. Beneath the shower a fellow informed me he was blind in one eye: from a bicycling accident – a warning, I presumed, to keep clear of his lane. A postman, who arrived in spit 'n' polished boots, his jacket lapels studded with enamel badges, put on a pair of freshly laundered underpants every morning after his shower – I couldn't help ogling the man's hairless white body. A medic relayed the gruesome details of the previous day's surgery to anyone who would listen. Spending time on my own, without work to distract me, I noticed these things. The days I passed on the beach sleeping off my exhaustion in the sun; the same spot every day, near a family threesome, an oldish couple on a late summer holiday with their teenage daughter. I watched through hooded eyes the girl's movements. Her quick flicks and pulls to a tight turquoise bathing costume; the frown of over-plucked eyebrows at an encroaching football; the sheer luxury of her browning young body. Like a girl of years before in Rimini . . . Teresa Herbert: that's it. She as ludicrously shy as me, both too old for family holidays – neither of us wise enough to make a move.

I'm surprised Gran didn't spot things going wrong with Dinah, and warn me.

I questioned her about this in September. But she's too far gone, doesn't know real time any more – she thought I meant Clare Raybould. It's sad that Dinah doesn't exist for Gran, as Gran herself was the only member of my family Dinah held in respect. Mum Dinah merely felt sorry for.

All muddled in her head Gran talked, in a girl's voice, about her mother – as if it was her long-buried mother who was ill not she herself. Gran's contorted hands fussed at the neck of her nightie: 'Mum's calling for her tea. Forgot Mum's tea.'

There were moments of lucidity. Like when she asked me about my work, reminding me it was she who helped finance the Durham launch of *Phalanx*: my name in print for the first time; maudlin love poems on the loss of Susannah – nothing to be proud of, I'm afraid, nothing to suggest I'll be a decent writer. Gran always encouraged me to be different, to aspire to the extraordinary. It's Gran who taught me to hunt out oddities for articles. An early piece – I remember – on the Ephemera Society's triennial auction, held in a Berkshire rose garden. Cut-throat competition for folding table loads of throwaway art; including a collection of monogrammed paper napkins stacked by date and country in a score of cardboard boxes. It's from Gran I learnt to prize most highly achievements gained not through giftedness – natural seamanship, near photographic memory, good health, reasonable looks, etc – but by graft. I inherited from Gran a desire to make things difficult for myself.

What else drives me to abandon our amazing us?

Explains why I'm happy here in Highbury Grange, living in another's house. Nothing created and nothing, therefore, to destroy.

Christmas this year was the worst. Worse than last, when I expected every moment to hear from Kathy – which pulled me through the days. Christmas is the time for missing, the time when I most miss Dinah and her world.

I miss the rounds of exhibition previews: the excitement of red dots – half dots for reservations – breaking out, like a welcome epidemic, in glazed display cases; the heat, drink and chatter; the craft gossip. I miss the pizza parties afterwards; the companionship of Dinah's chums, and their admiration of my writing.

This Christmas I felt excluded from a world – the Pollard family circle – to which I'd expected always to be centrally attached.

I even caught myself missing Barry Macdonald, I'm ashamed to admit.

Barry's grand celebration at Fordingham Castle feels like

yesterday, our us as solid as a rock. I can't believe we won't be at the next one . . . that I won't. Dinah will – with another man? It's their sense of occasion I admire, the ability of those people to make necessity fun, their skill at giving themselves treats. Barry doesn't need to fill his country house hotels with friends for free weekends, it's just an excuse for a party (to test the system before opening to the public: he tactfully maintains to those – like me – who are embarrassed about not paying). He does it with such style, so lavishly: champagne in a bucket of ice in every bedroom; the porters in green overalls, like family retainers. Barry numbered two ex-Cabinet Ministers, several City dignitaries, the Director of British Heritage and a *Nine O'Clock News* presenter amongst his friends for the Fordingham weekend. Somebody from Sotheby's led a guided tour of the house before we changed for dinner.

Our suite boasted an enormous bath, big enough for the two of us. We drank our champagne together in the bath, I remember.

Hard to believe all this is over: the past, packed away in the attic.

Cullum Jones – the British Heritage man – made a fool of himself. A group gathered in the hall of the Castle on the Sunday morning, ready for a walk through the snow-covered grounds.

'Damn. Didn't think of Wellingtons,' Cullum complained.

'I brought mine,' his wife beamed.

'Please darling, don't be frivolous. They won't fit me,' he barked.

We all laughed like drains – and he'd no idea why, poor fellow.

It's not the individuals I miss so much as the ambience, the air of importance, of belonging. Take the Vollmers. I don't miss daily contact with Gus and Fifi for themselves but for the connection. I miss the comfort of their knowing, effortlessly, what I'm up to, where I'm at. Who I am. Their knowing meant I knew too. These days I have to rely on my own sense of self. Yes, you're Alastair Shore, the journalist: I tell myself. Recently separated from your wife. (How recent's recent?) In love with a girl you never see. Waiting for your divorce so she'll feel free to be with you.

I can't rid my mind of the idea that Dinah has extracted a promise from Kathy not to make contact with me during the two years of legal separation.

They're both capable of it.

Kathy is tough enough to wish to have nothing to do with me unless I can find, in myself, the courage to trust her.

Which I do. Readily. I understand what her silence means. Her saying nothing says everything. If she wanted me to forget about her she'd tell me so, instead of staying silent.

I've said it all before, I know. Dozens of times. I repeat myself over and over again. It seems I have to, that it's all part of the process.

No use not doubting, is there? Otherwise there'd be no test.

I've faced up to Dinah's awesome hurt, as well.

Death is a sharp pinch compared with this continuous grinding, twisting, tearing, wrenching of my softest most tender guts.

Dinah's words again, my wife's refrain.

I take it all and still go forward.

I'm haunted at the moment by a boyhood memory. It keeps recurring, after years of hibernation, and I can't see what connection it has to anything of the present. Or rather: I don't see why this particular memory comes back, day by day, in preference to others.

It incorporates two overlapping scenes, each involving table tennis.

We used to keep the table tennis table at one end of the garage. When Auntie Sylvia, Cheryll and Roland came for the day, after tea we'd all troop into the garage for a game of round-the-table. The garage was cold, smelt of carburettor oil and cat litter.

'The aim is to keep the rallies going. Not to win,' my father instructs. 'Three lives each. Two practice rounds.' Dozens of times though Auntie Sylvia has played the game, she still manages to make mistakes. She forgets, in her satisfaction at making the return, to discard the bat for the next player; and dithers between ends when play starts, invariably deciding to go the wrong way. Cheryll and I giggle at her mother's feebleness. Whilst Dad becomes more and more irritated by breaks in play, scuttling after the ball like a spider, bony limbs precariously attached to his stoop-shouldered torso.

'Concentrate Sylvia, for God's sake.'

'Language, language. Never hear you speak to Mary like that,' his sister responds, nodding at Mum.

In the second remembered scene, still in the garage, Dad and I are playing on our own. We're testing out a new pair of Sorbot bats, Dad standing back while I practice smashes. 'Good, good. Very good,' he says. We play a match; the best of three, as usual. He wins the first. Me the second. In the third I'm winning – and I can tell he's trying his hardest – a point or two, only, separating us all the way up to twenty/nineteen. And then it happens. I'm just about to serve. And it happens. I can't hold it in any more. The warm piss flows down my legs, into my shoes and in a darkening puddle out over the concrete floor.

Dad looks nervously at the door to the scullery. 'Won't tell your mother,' he whispers.

He gets an old towel from the boot of the car to mop up the floor. Tells me to take off my trousers and socks, which he wrings out and I put back on.

'We'll go for a drive,' he decides.

I remember Dad with greater affection that afternoon than at any other time in my whole life. We were conspirators: me holding myself close to the fan heater to dry out; he dumping the incriminating towel in a municipal dustbin.

I wasn't so young. Already boarding at Hillhead.

My shoes weren't quite dry when we returned home, though luckily Mum never noticed. She never said anything, anyway.

Mary and Stephen Shore married and made love in the spring of 1944: she with a rush of fear that the world might be extinguished, permanently blacked-out, without her having known a man; he in instantaneous adoration. Staff Officer Mary Biddle – as she then was – met her tall Flight Lieutenant, a navigator of Hercules bombers, on a Monday and married him on the Friday, two days before he returned to his squadron in Norfolk. Their time together during the last year of the War was limited to snatched encounters at halfway meeting places – overcrowded railway hotels mostly – and in those dangerous days Mary loved her husband, took pride in opening her body to him. Enjoyed his exaltation.

Mary's was a responsible War. Joining the WRAF straight from school in South London, she blossomed into one of the airforce's finest map-makers, responsible, by the end, for draughting operational maps for many of the most delicate missions. Despite her youth and the frailty of her physical appearance she earned a reputation for tireless dependability, nothing was too much for her in the course of duty. Even when a stray bomb fell on the house in Mitcham where she was born, brought up and still lived, killing both her parents – a mistake, she presumed, the nervousness of some young German airman on his way in to the City targets – Mary was back at work a day later. In all this suffering Mary learnt that work, her satisfaction in being good at it, kept her cheerful. She was pleased also to find that in advancing her career faster than most of her contemporaries she nevertheless retained their friendship. This mattered to her: the earning of her peers' respect a dominant force in Mary's wartime life of dedication. Daily confronting the pain of death, she noticed the varied strengths and frailties of human nature: in men as in women, flyers and ground staff, officers and crew. Pilots who drowned their fears in drink, WRAF colleagues who gave themselves nightly in the backs of motor cars, Mary Shore judged no one, forgave everyone everything in the happiness of discovering the capacity within herself to win respect.

With the War almost won Stephen and Mary were reunited:

in the bombing of Dresden. Attached to Central Command, Mary helped map the bomber squadron's complex paths of flight into the industrial heartland of Germany; and it was she, in a sense, who therefore guided Stephen to his seventh medal.

After demobilisation the couple set up home near Stephen's family in York, where he secured a promising post in the Borough Architect's Department. Until becoming pregnant with Alastair, Mary occupied her time in voluntary work at the Cathedral, and although she made no conscious decision, worked nothing out in her head, she found herself setting out to build, brick by brick, a barrier between all that went before and everything which was to follow. Nothing of the War was allowed to survive the Armistice, the living memory of those years buried with the dead behind an impenetrable wall of silence. The War changed everything for Mary, nothing could be the same again – would ever be allowed to. Look where wartime life pitched her up in the end: at the destruction of Dresden, inarguable proof – Mary learnt from those horrific photographs – of human failure, of man's inhumanity to man. The part she had uncritically played in the Dresden massacre left Mary feeling, in an almost child-like way, let down. She felt misled. Misused. Made a fool of: in allowing herself to believe that anything she did mattered, that her doing things well made any difference. When Alastair was born Mary promised to protect the child from a similar fate. She vowed to equip her beautiful boy with the ability, first and foremost, never to lose control of his own destiny, to be so perfectly self-disciplined that nothing could upset his balance. It became her passion, this modelling of a son. Whilst needing to conceal from him knowledge of the precise awfulness which drove her own certainty, wishing him spared awareness of exactly what the dangers were against which he must be protected, she brought him up to be forever vigilant. Why? the boy tried to ask. For reasons too ghastly-black to tell: Mary's harsh looks and clipped commands and quick squeezes of the hand replied.

Her young mother's love for the child bubbled inside just as boilingly for Alastair the man. Mary had recognised within moments of his birth that the love she felt for her son reduced other emotions to ashes. She knew she should love her husband, was meant to reward his adoration with womanly warmth; she wanted, for her own sake, to do so – but could not. She hoped the creation of another child might raise in her the correct response – but it did not. It made her feel yet guiltier: for loving her son with exclusive passion. No one else could compete with Alastair's looks, his double-banked rows of eyelashes longer, more beautiful than his sister's; with Alastair's strength, his broad-chested, stocky-limbed figure more dependable than his father's; with Alastair's intelligence, sensitivity and loyalty; with his integrity; with his authenticity. . . Not that she let him guess the boundless extent of this love for him, lest he relax his guard and get hurt. Mary did not curry love but maintained instead, however heart-strong the questioning appeal in her son's stare, her controlling concern and constancy of emotional restraint. You know I love you, my darling: the brush of her fingers through his hair said more eloquently than any words. You know I'd die for you if it would do any good – death for life. But the world doesn't work like that, so simply. You're on your own, I can teach you only to be careful.

Safety, however, was the minimum requirement, the baseline of Mary's ambition for Alastair. She actually wanted – and fully expected – much more of him than mere survival.

Mary's discipline at home was not designed to tie her children permanently to her side. Quite the reverse. Far from wishing Alastair to live life on her behalf, Mary hoped for his escape to a better existence entirely of his own making. She did not need her son to be like her. The point, the whole purpose of the struggle, of the striving, was for Alastair to grow up knowing himself to be as good as the next man, rather than worrying – as she did, all the time – about what next would go wrong.

Conscious of her own social unease, Mary was determined to educate her son to feel confident of his ability to perform: in all circumstances, under any pressure. The right way to behave was to come naturally to him, his manners so well drilled he need never stop to think. Mary's moment of triumph – recompense for twenty-five year's relentless control, of herself as well as of the family – arrived with Alastair's wedding day. The marriage of her son to Dinah Pollard when first broached seemed too implausibly wonderful to contemplate: beyond a mother's wildest dreams. She dared not believe it was happening;

expected every second a rude awakening, the failure – in some ritual the secret of which she did not know to tell – of her son to pass the test. The very second Alastair rose to take his place in the aisle the Vicar of Godstow stepped forward. A frown distorted the cleric's cheery face, and Mary's heart missed a beat. 'What's he saying? I can't hear what he's saying,' she gasped. But nothing went wrong. Alastair carried himself off perfectly, and his mother allowed herself to shed a public tear of pride. He made a lovely speech at the reception, short and tasteful, with none of his father's smutty jokes.

'You've met the groom's mother?' Phillip Pollard introduced her to the county guests.

The groom's mother? That's me, she pinched herself. Only happens once, might as well enjoy it.

Alastair's father-in-law, with his overfed cheeks and the ostentatious wiping of his nose on a silk handkerchief, was just the type to make Mary feel at her least secure. (Not that she allowed such feelings to show: habitual concealment of anxiety so effective many people were themselves afraid of her.) In the event Mary was charmed by Mr Pollard, a man who had taught himself how to treat women, knew where on their bodies to place a guiding hand, when to do it and how long to leave it there. What she found particularly attractive was his openness. The obvious pleasure he derived from women rendered his judicious caresses, the low-toned flatteries, the sensuous little wettings of his lips with the pink tip of his tongue, enchanting. In their ritual perambulation of the wedding marquee Mary found herself feeling, for the first time in many years, that mothers were women, were feminine. Phillip Pollard made her feel like a proper woman.

The centre of Mary's satisfaction that triumphal day rested, however, with her son. Her pleasure in the intuitive conviction that Alastair would find happiness with Dinah was intense. Although she declined to see it as such. The champagne-fuelled excitement she felt was distinctly sexual. In her limitingly romantic imagination Mary saw Dinah sweep Alastair off his feet and ride away with him on the back of a winged white horse: to make love on the hot sand of a secret beach, sheer cliffs at their back, the break of waves at their feet, gulls lolling on the summer air.

Mary let thrive in the love of her son all the cajoling dreamy subtlety which – sadly – she had never directed to herself. She knew his body more intimately than her own. Knew the shape of every inch of him – the precise knobbliness of his knees. She knew him physically as a man not merely as a child; watched, fascinated, as fans of hair spread out over the flesh of his tummy and chest; saw the first folds of age appear at his lower eyelids; noticed the adult tightening of muscles at the base of his neck, a hunching of the shoulders. Mary reacted to her son's passage from adolescence to adulthood as if it were her own, fearing for him as she had once feared for herself – only more so, because by then experience had taught her how real the dangers were. Mary prayed for his finding the courage to let go, to abandon himself to love.

Dinah – Mary believed – was the answer to these prayers. With Dinah Alastair might sing while making love, not silently cry as Mary almost always had, in sorrow at the repeated nothingness. Alerted to the problem by his teenage acne, Mary was aware of Alastair's unease with girls. The eruptions on her son's trim cheeks worried her, for the spots looked sore as well as ugly, not pimples but fat headless boils. Alastair's acne lasted so long and inflicted such a deep scarring to his face Mary took him to a London skin specialist, who informed her – at thirty pounds an hour – that there was nothing to be done bar cosmetic easing of the inelegance. Part of growing up: they all insisted, a difficulty some boys suffered where others were spared, depending, largely, on attitudes to sex. Already? Mary queried. Already at fifteen years old her Alastair's life marred by sexuality? How unfair. Was there nothing she could do to help?

She heard (from the girl's mother) of Alastair's mooning about the fields near Lizzie Thomas'. Mary – who had herself been a pretty teenager, early into her woman's body – felt for Lizzie, pitied the girl the silliness her beauty was destined to inspire in men: in Alastair already, evidently. Clare Raybould, the tarty daughter of a local GP, was a more suitable first girlfriend. Bound to be on the pill, Mary reckoned. (She remembered catching Alastair and Clare kissing in the garage when they were meant to be playing table tennis, and being impressed by the girl's stare of unrepentant defiance). Mary lied

– not a lie, exactly, more of a semi-truth – to Dr Raybould about Alastair's job in the South of France, pretending her son lodged with French family friends in Toulon when she knew perfectly well he and a pal from school were living unchaperoned on a houseboat across the bay in St Mandrier. Whatever happened during Clare's three week holiday with Alastair in the sun it clearly pleased neither of them; for Mary saw instantly on the girl's return the dissatisfaction in her face, the corners of her mouth set sour for life. With Alastair she sensed rather than saw a parallel disillusionment heightening her anxiety for his future happiness.

It was perverse of her, contradictory, she acknowledged, to hope for Alastair's happiness given the bleak outlook of her own example, the necessity for caution beamed at him since birth. Happiness for Mary had ceased years before to be a possibility; so long ago that memories of joyful moments in her youth which from time to time floated into consciousness felt as though they belonged to somebody else, part of another's life, a stranger's childhood in the suburbs of South London.

The only images of pleasure from the past which Mary recognised as properly relating to herself involved Alastair. He was the source – the joy was her child's, his to share with his grateful mother; joy plucked from the air itself, manufactured in chubby fistfuls of grass, an empty plastic cup, the car keys. Her baby's skill at laughter astonished Mary.

Aware somewhere at the back of her mind that the Mitcham girl, the stranger from her past, had also liked them Mary made a speciality of children's picnics. All the Shore's best family times were associated with picnics, the tartan car rug – a christening present from Wilf – spread out on top of an old RAF groundsheet, the stink of Stephen's pipe less offensive, she found, in the open air. 'I'm not carting any of this stuff back home,' she used to say, her voice raised in threatened anger, daring them – it would appear – to waste her efforts (in fact, saving herself the later sense of pointlessness in unpacking uneaten picnic food). Once, unobserved, crouching behind some gorse bushes in a headland ravine above Robin Hood's Bay, she witnessed Alastair's discovery of a sheep's carcase, recently dead, flies buzzing in the hollow eyes, guts half-eaten. He was six at the time, his face tanned in the sea-sun, near the end of their two-week break with Stephen's mother. He looked around to check he was alone, then squatted on his haunches beside the animal's body, eyebrows drawn together in concentration. He put out his hand. The hand hovered above the rank yellow fleece; touched and pulled back; touched again – less frantically, more feelingly. Alastair smiled to himself, straightened, and ran on along the sheep-track. Mary watched him go, as content as he with his independence, delighted with this unforced proof of her son's sufficiency. When they met up later at the picnic spot – Wilf's rug already folded away, strapped to the back of the wicker hamper – she wondered if he would tell of his adventure, and felt a surge of pride at her child's decision to keep the secret to himself.

The removal of any hope of fulfilment in her own life she blamed on Stephen. Mental cruelty (a term culled from an article on divorce in the *Sunday Telegraph*) was the way Mary best liked to describe the problem, in imagined conversations with her phantom confidante. Stephen systematically undermined her in public, she complained, his inattention forcing her into less and less reasonable – laughable, even – exaggerations in order to make her voice heard. None of the Shore entourage in York took her seriously. She could tell by the way friends referred to him for confirmation: of her Church Fellowship anecdotes; of school-run schedules; of directions to a restaurant. They all – some without bothering to disguise their doubts, others in more subtly superior ways – turned to Stephen for notice whether or not she was to be believed. And Stephen, instead of supporting her, played their game.

Money matters were a particular weakness of Mary's, not having earned or owned a penny since demobilisation at the end of the War. Stephen handled all their financial affairs – paying bills, organising life insurance, coping with the school fees, deciding when and where they could afford a holiday . . . adding, automatically, extra cash at New Year to her weekly allowance: to buy Sarah-Jane and Alastair clothes in the sales. At first, immersed in motherhood, she accepted as normal her dependence on him for money, let him feel she felt protected. 'Don't worry, I'll deal with that,' he would say, removing from her once capable hands another piece of paper – the water rates, or a voters' registration form – puffing all the while at his pipe.

Later, without understanding quite what it was she found so objectionable, doubting in her heart her right to complain, to demand to know, Mary grew to despise her own ignorance.

There was nothing she could do about it: which further maddened her; and reduced her in the end to hating him. 'Honestly Mary, you haven't a clue what you're talking about.' Of *course* she hadn't. How could she? He proved her wrong every time, even when she knew, deep inside that she was right – merely lacked the means, the experience, the words to defend her point-of-view. Mary hated Stephen for his bland indifference to her predicament, his refusal to take her frustration seriously. 'You've no reason to worry,' he assured her. Why couldn't he tell her how it worked then, explain to her the system, let her see for herself everything really was in order? Reason or not, she did worry – couldn't he accept that? She hated him for maintaining his own steady pattern of work and recreation, unaffected – he claimed – by her outbursts. 'Look, it's you who's upset, not me. What can I do? You exaggerate. There's nothing to worry about, I promise.'

'Men don't have women's problems,' Stephen once mumblingly commented. 'And what do you mean by that remark?' she challenged, silencing his hesitant attempt to broach the subject of sex. For this she blamed him too: for his failure to break the taboo and help her face her sexuality. When pressed he pretended not to mind about their limited love-life, never attempting force. Somewhere within his vital inner recesses Stephen was scared of her, she came to realise. The fact that he clearly tried his best to be kind and was, in truth, a far from cruel man made her feel bad for blaming him, guilty for not being happier.

But who else was there to blame?

Left to herself everything would have been different – better, she did not doubt. Mental cruelty: that was how marriage felt to Mary Shore.

Mary considered her son to be weak too in certain ways, like his father. There was real danger, also, in Alastair's strengths, his successes. More so in success perhaps than failure, in the dependence inherent in his taste for being admired. She had diagnosed Alastair's susceptibility to success already as an adolescent, anticipating nothing but hurt to follow disappointment of his swollen-headed expectations. It pained her to react negatively to his achievements, to see his bright eyes cloud in bewilderment at failure to elicit her approval. Praise would go to his head. Praise would replace self-sufficiency with a craving for company, make an introvert into a show-off. Mary pushed him to do well at school in order to better his defence not, in lap-dog pleasure at attention, to lay himself open to hurt. Schoolboy success left Alastair more vulnerable not less: his mother learnt, the lesson repeated a decade later when *The British City* made him marginally famous. It was nice, of course, when the Dean's wife billowed across the Close to congratulate her, announcing – for all to hear – that the Dean and she never missed a programme. 'Isn't Alastair doing well for himself?' they clucked at the hairdresser's. Was he, she had wondered? Doing well and being well were not the same thing at all. She doubted the quality of his pleasure, the result of public accolade not necessarily a reflection of what he felt inside. She feared he would be punished for stepping out of line and daring to be distinguished.

Alastair was too easily influenced by things he read, ever parading the efficacy of his newest enthusiasm; and too easily swayed too by the opinions of his friends, women in particular (like snobby Susannah, who had thrown him overboard for a better catch). Her son was ripe picking, Mary angrily observed, for the pretty Jewish mischief-maker at Roxeth House. Why did Jews always stick their noses into other people's business? Give opinions no one asked to hear? They professed to be concerned solely with securing due respect, when primarily engaged in asserting their superiority. Mary could not stop herself secretly believing – despite her dislike of the Germans – that the Jews must somehow have provoked attack, that they deserved, after centuries of profiteering, their fate. Why else did so few raise a hand in their semitic neighbour's defence, and thousands – tens of thousands – participate uncomplainingly in their slaughter? They must have had their reasons: Mary maintained.

Alastair inherited his feebleness with women directly from his father: that at least was clear – together with Stephen's nose, a sharp head for finance, his interest in architecture, and many other undeniable similarities, most of which his mother resented. Both men, for example, wanted to paint the house white – all the walls, ceilings and doors, in all the rooms – whilst Mary favoured pastel woodwork and patterned wallpaper, liked regularly to redecorate in step with the lastest nostalgic revival. 'Go ahead, if it makes you happy,' Stephen always agreed, spoiling it by adding, 'looks perfectly all right to me, I must say.' She had expected Alastair to grow up to be her ally, the bearer home with her of carpet samplebooks and vinyl-silk colour charts, laid out on the dining table and together mined for matching combinations. Alastair's adult echo, phrase by phrase, of his father's taste hurt Mary more than she cared to admit. The injustice – and insult – of Alastair's desertion turned her stomach. Didn't he remember how his father tormented him with the black dog teasings? Mary did. Mary remembered the boy's contorted face, white in silent rage, and his embittered smile on being forced in the end to take it as a joke. Remembered her own agony in permitting Stephen's pursuit – knowing the importance of Alastair's learning to make himself invulnerable – of his acquiring the knack of shrugging taunts aside.

It was Mary who met Alastair off the train at York on his visits north. Always early, she invariably parked in the same place: in the far corner by the coalyard fence, where she felt the car was least likely to be bumped. Patient on the platform, facing down the line to London, Mary pushed aside the usual fear – silly in itself, she knew, but nevertheless upsetting – that Alastair might have taken to smoking a pipe. The loosening flesh of her lower lip trembled at the unwelcome image of her son's leap from the train, a bulbous briar pipe stuck between his teeth. No, surely not. Mary pressed a hand to her hat-pin, then brushed fingers through her grey fringe, regretting the decision fifteen years or so before, when the ageing could no longer be ignored, not to dye her hair. Other women gathered on the platform; Mary knew several, and felt obliged to exchange smiles, but turned her moist eyes resolutely away from conversation. The sight of Alastair's bare head in the crush of travellers, the unfussy touch of her lips to his cheek, his 'Hello Mum', delivered in a deep adult voice, never disappointed. Whatever new sadnesses coloured their lives apart, the brief together-time in the act of greeting made up for everything.

Why? Mary asked herself. Because the sense of Alastair's intimate presence in the public dirt and bustle of a railway station redefined him as hers, confirmed it truly was she who had made him. For nine-and-a-half safe months inside and eleven more outside at her breasts she had fed every fibre of his body and being. He was entirely hers, she his: their meeting off the train affirmed.

Their connectedness was also a source of regret to Mary. He, like her, had no one to talk to. She since the War and the loss of contact with her friends in the WRAF; he – for fewer years numerically but a larger slice of life – since the break-up of his boyhood gang of three. He, she imagined, talked his troubles through with himself – just as she did: seldom getting anywhere. Alastair was worse than her, she had noticed, at asking for help. In simple things: the time from a passer-by in the street; or to borrow a neighbour's programme at the theatre. If he disliked asking directions to the toilets in a department store, how could he dare open up his heart?

Unable to be intimate: was that why he ran away from Dinah?

Mary doubted her capacity, however long she might live, fully to understand why her son abandoned his wife. Something irreplaceably precious, her favourite day-dream, died the second she accepted Alastair's marriage was over. She suffered twice, a double loss: first for him and second, once his survival was assured, for herself. Mary loved Dinah more than Sarah-Jane, her own daughter. She loved Dinah selfishly, in pleasure at the girl's spontaneous hugs and kisses, at the mutual sharing of their joy in Alastair. Dinah dared order Mary – in her own home – to sit down and relax, put her feet up. Didn't just tell her to relax, like Stephen was constantly doing, but helped her to, showed her how. It was such an extraordinary experience: to receive the outright gift of Dinah's love, nothing demanded in return. To feel loved for who she was, for the things she most valued in herself.

Mary did not blame Dinah for turning from love to abuse when Alastair broke his vow and fled. The vitriolic letters Dinah sent, religiously, to York at Christmas were calculated to hurt – and so they did. The language itself shocked, a crude screech of pain across the page. Dinah's anger and confusion, her wild, thrashing, smashing search for something, someone to punish for what had happened to her – out-of-the-blue, defenceless, all argument denied – made more sense to Mary than Alastair's aloof control. She felt guilty not merely on her son's behalf but in herself; guilty by default. Mary blamed herself for not warning Dinah, months before the storm broke, of Alastair's muddled state. She had seen his steady strengthening of emotional barriers, and said nothing. Several times she almost spoke . . . but the possibility of their splitting up never occurred to her . . . No. Better not interfere, she told herself – for fear of offending Dinah, of losing her love. They've had an argument. About babies, probably. It'll blow over.

It was foolish, Mary now realised, to have imagined she existed for Dinah as a person in her own right, distinct from being Alastair's mother. It was not she the Pollards seemed to like, appeared to make welcome at family festivities in Godstow, it was their daughter's mother-in-law. Otherwise they would have continued to invite her down to those wonderful weekends, wouldn't they?

Not a word, though. No letter of regret. No conciliatory phonecalls. No parental collusion to mend the break. Nothing.

She saw, in her darkened day-dream, Phillip Pollard cross out her telephone number in his pocket book.

After months of toing and froing – Dinah agreeing such-and-such was fair, then demanding more – putting my signature to our separation papers was a relief. I'll never again sit with her in Blackheath and suffer her hurt, was all I could think of. On signature of the official separation Dinah's pain became her own, mine my own. We were no longer responsible for each other, the agreement stated.

I felt no regret. Just relief.

My solicitor, Sheila Bowman, poured me a glass of celebratory sherry. 'Cheers,' she said. 'That's the least contentious settlement I've ever handled.'

Crippling according to Susannah – Susannah says Dinah took advantage of my guilty conscience to cripple me. Maybe she has financially, I don't mind. I just want it all to be over. 'You'd chuck me out of my home as well? You hate me that much?' Dinah hurled at me. No, I couldn't do that to her. Making a home, the feathering of our nest, had been so important to her – seemed to be to me too, at one time. I've changed. I honestly don't care about having a home. She can keep it all, I'll be all right. I just want to get on with my life.

Over sherry I tried to make Sheila understand. She didn't, of course. Slightly older than me – how much it's difficult to tell beneath the layers of make-up, uniform each day – she had recently become engaged to a senior partner in the firm of solicitors on the floor below, and almost glowed.

I gave up. 'Good luck,' I said, gulped my drink and fled.

I don't remember actually feeling anything. I felt nothing,

in fact. That's where the relief came: in *not* feeling. To be numb.

Nothing had happened. Signing a piece of paper didn't alter anything – any more than the rigmarole of our wedding had. No point in getting upset about it; we were through to the final leg, that was all it meant. Plain sailing from there on in, I imagined.

I suppose the only way men survive the trauma of their broken marriages is by assuming that each wave of pain as it breaks over them is the last, that the storm is spent? Like the meeting in Blackheath when we finally agreed terms. That's it. It's over now. Everything will get better now: I thought.

Dinah had packed the woven love-dolls into a shoe box, cushioned in a bed of cotton wool, and wouldn't let me leave without them. She wrapped her arms tight around my waist, pressed her face close beneath my chin and licked my neck.

'Your taste. I wanted to taste you, for the last time,' she said.

I couldn't bring myself to kiss her on the mouth – so she licked the sweat from my neck instead. When I made for the door, muttering some lame cliché or another – 'Take care', or something – Dinah told me she was seeing a psychiatrist.

'Don't worry about me. I'm in therapy now. Yes, very interesting. You should try it. Might make you better in bed. And don't kid yourself it's going to be different with Kathy,' she went on. 'You speak of her like you used to of me. The same old thing. You'll mess that up too unless you sort yourself out.'

I couldn't – still can't – make sense of it: the licking, her gift of the dolls, this strange speech. My Dinah, so disturbed that she needs therapy?

'Oh, yes. You'd better hand over your keys,' she said on the doorstep.

Dinah hurts me most when she's least angry. Standing in the rain in the stable yard (Fifi peering – probably – from behind her kitchen curtains) I had to fish in my briefcase for the keys to my own house and drop them into my wife's open hand. She smiled, and closed the door.

Signing the separation papers themselves was nothing after that. A release. A relief: as I've said.

What worries me is that I never seem able to get things straight in my head, to put anything in order. With my feelings clear how come my thoughts remain in such a muddle?

Nothing settles. Nothing finds a permanent place. I work like a madman at it, scribbling away, pummelling ideas into a semblance of order – and then something happens to pitch the whole lot into chaos again. Contact with Dinah, usually. She telephones in distress late at night. Or writes a letter – upbeat and hopeful:

> It's a miracle. The symbiosis is broken. The chords cut and we are weaned off each other. It's a miracle. We have come through, but above all, we have come through without losing love and respect for each other. It's a miracle . . . I will always understand, my love, always. Please don't stop trusting me.

What am I meant to make of that?

I can't rid myself of a picture in my mind of us in our old age, in Scarborough, Dinah pushing me along the promenade in a cane bath-chair, Mum's tartan rug warming my knees. I can't help believing, when the game's over, when I've proved to myself whatever it is I'm trying to, that we'll end our time together. Exactly as we've always dreamed.

She loves me, you see. She'll never be able fully to give herself to anyone else: she says. She is literally mine forever. There's no escape: Dinah says.

Who am I to deny her right to love? Why should I want to?

Too little love, not too much, is what hurts. Everyone needs to know they are loved. I'm no exception.

Maybe it's not true? Maybe one can be over-loved, wrongly loved anyway?

Until death us do part: the Vicar of Godstow made us promise. Our once sacred us!

Death doesn't frighten me. I'd prefer not to die right now (not yet, such a lot still to achieve) but the idea doesn't frighten me – Mrs Appleton's hell-fires, and all that. Like war. I'd have been a hero in the War, brave and unflappable, repeatedly risking life and limb.

It's the thought of others' death I can't stand, the threat of being left behind to mourn. I once made Dinah promise – seriously, not in play – to let me die first, and she agreed: 'No, you wouldn't be much use without me. Would you, Woolly?' It's odd the way that sounds, now that it's written down, more like base fear than bravery; instead of paralysing me goads me into self-protective action, inspires me to do before I'm done to. Maybe that's what makes heroes of men: the unknown dangers outside easier to face than known fears inside; death a better bet than survival. Maybe that's what Dinah means when she says she'd rather I were dead, than alive and not hers.

The only dead body I've seen was floating in the sea beneath Bridlington Pier, trapped along with planks of wood, tar-blacked fenders and a beach ball in the tidal eddies between the piers. We went after the beach ball, spotted through the slats . . . Charlie went after it, to be accurate – Jonty and I followed. The entire day was Charlie's creation, he arranged the whole thing: consulted the train timetable; plied our parents for permission; took out junior membership of Bridlington Angling Association so we could fish free from the pier. Charlie even made my rod, when Mum refused to buy me one. If Charlie was the leader, Jonty the brains, who was I? The dreamer? I'm not sure I won more than a dozen games of noughts and crosses against Jonty in all the hundreds of times we must have played. He knew what he was aiming at, had memorised the lethal configurations which made victory inevitable. Jonty planned ahead whilst I muddled along turn-by-turn, defeating his strategies on occasion by luck not judgement. At school we all considered Jonty brilliant – Christ knows whether he was or not; or what, if anything, he's done with it . . . The dead man floated face down in the water, a pillow of air trapped in the shoulders of his mackintosh keeping him at the surface. He was close enough to the iron stairs down which we'd clambered for us to have reached out to grab his hair and pull him in. But we didn't – even Charlie baulked at that, and dispatched Jonty to call the Police. 'Clear off, there's good lads. Been in the water some time, won't be a pretty sight,' a policeman warned. I obeyed – and have regretted doing so ever since; for Charlie and Jonty, who stayed to watch, know what it looks like to be dead, whereas I can only dream.

I think of death as a mask hiding the emptiness left behind by the man who was once inside. We all wear masks at times (all the time, some of us) and they usually denote our absence; or at best a pretence only at presence. Susannah says I looked like death during the early months after leaving Dinah – but I can't remember feeling dead at all. I remember feeling very much alive, in myself. I suppose I'd stopped pretending to be there when I wasn't. A moving on to the new life, letting go of the old. Letting go is giving birth, I read somewhere.

My father is a master at pretending to be attentive when he's miles away – he's got to be, to repel the lash of Mum's invective. He has to ignore the hateful things she says to him – in order to survive. Neither of them seem to notice the ugliness of their constant confrontations. They accept their quarrelling as a fact of life, immutable, closed to negotiation. Mum uses my visits north to bolster her attack, storing up petty complaints to voice while I'm there to take her side. Mum assumes I'm an ally, that I'll back her up. And I do: she's right. I almost always do.

'This man is *so stupid*,' she spits – the three of us ensconced in the drawing room sipping tea.

Dad takes it all without a murmur of dissent, a flicker, merely, of distaste in his mask-like eyes . . . Actually, that's not true. Years ago he used to answer back, try to tease her out of these mad exaggerations and make her smile. I've proof – in black and white. In my album there's a snap of Dad, Mum and me taken in Trafalgar Square, with pigeons eating corn from the crown of Dad's trilby. And Mum is laughing; that's the point – when a minute before she was dragging us away from the smarmy street photographer. 'What's the harm in it? Nice to have a record of the day,' Dad countered. Despite Mum's murderous looks Dad persevered – and I've the photo to prove it: that he was once able to make her happy.

I know they love each other. My parents must surely love each other; it's being friends they find difficult.

The *decree nisi* went through today. Two years. We haven't

'co-habited' for two years. Can it be? There's a part of me which feels as though I left her last weekend; and another part which feels we've never met. Dinah Pollard and my Woolly: are they the same person? Doesn't seem possible.

I forgive you, my love, all the vile things you've said to me. You didn't mean them, I know you didn't mean them.

There's nothing more I can do or say or write to convince you of your blamelessness. It's over. I've done it; and it's done.

I must get it straight in my head.

Dinah and I had the wrong kind of love. There's nothing the matter with her in herself, nor me in myself, nor love in itself, it's the way we loved which was wrong.

It wasn't love at all, not really, not from my side; for me the real reason for being with her was need, giant need. If I hadn't needed Dinah so desperately maybe I could have loved her – it's sad to have ruined, by now, any chance of finding out. We thought we loved each other, told ourselves we did, convinced everyone else we'd found the magic answer, although we hadn't at all. Instead of loving Dinah I created a monster love of our us: that's what happened. And when I saw the creature for who he was, a fraud, a trickster, a cheat, not a rock but a balloon, I pricked his belly and he burst. BANG! Nothing left, except the damp rubber of discarded need.

I'm not being cruel, I'm being truthful; true to myself.

It's simpler to list the things I don't want from love than to name the things I do.

I don't want ever again to push away love – Dinah pressing herself against me; me pushing her away – I never want to feel that feeling again: of self-disgust, basically.

I don't want to have to pretend to a single thing any more.

I never again want not to be certain I'm doing right. I want to cut out permanently the wondering if people are pleased with me – not only Dinah, others too: my mother, for instance. Mum most of all, probably. Mum breathes tension into everything – take her picnics, spoiled for me by my terror of breaking the thermos flask. She broke one herself once – I can hear the popping sound, and see the millions of shiny slivers of glass – and although Mum made light of her doing it, I knew how upset she'd always be if I did. Glass kills, she used to say. Tiny bits of glass get washed by the blood in your veins up to your heart and get stuck. Stop your heart beating. Bits of glass smaller than you can see. Less than a pin-prick, and a week later you're dead.

I don't want not to want children. It's such a chilling feeling, not wanting your wife to be a mother: it mustn't ever happen to me again.

In the garden the other day Sarah-Jane picked up Emma and gave her a gratuitous hug. Secure in her mother's arms the woman-to-be smiled at the girl-that-was – while they held each other's gaze in limitless delight for what seemed an eternity. 'What love,' I remarked – to which Emma responded by pressing her nose into my sister's hair and squeezing her chubby arms ever tighter about Sarah-Jane's neck. This is how Dinah and I imagined we loved. But we didn't. We loved an idea, not each other.

There's no hurry with love: that's the crucial lesson Kathy has taught me.

It's over two years since I last saw her and my young love has grown, not withered. Give it time: I've millions of times reminded myself she said. I realise, finally, I've nothing to fear from time – that time is love's friend. Time and love love and time, ever entwined, are lovers.

I admire Kathy for daring to stay silent. She knows I must be sure who I am for myself regardless of whoever she thinks I might be. Same for her. She's taken this time for herself as well as giving it to me. I understand now what she was saying in Greenwich Park on my birthday . . .

If only I could be as certain in my heart as I am in my head. My heart fears, sometimes, that Kathy might be a coward, not a saint. That Kathy may lack the courage to confront me face-to-face and tell me it was all a mistake, that she was merely flirting.

Is Kathy Abraham no better than a little flirt?

Was our 'love' meant to have been an ordinary affair, its allotted span of time long since expired?

Four forty-four and twenty-eight seconds. Wait . . . There! 4.44.44!

I love it when that happens, when I glance down at my watch and all the numbers are about to coincide. Dates too – though dates are much rarer: once in a decade only. You have to plan ahead to catch the digital dates. 8.8.88 – the eighth of August nineteen eighty-eight – is the next.

At 8.88.88 on 8.8.88: twice in one day, morning and evening.

That'll be the time to be together.